Ari, I hope this is gruesome enough for you!

THE O'MALLEY & SWIFT CRIME THRILLERS

Corn Dolls

Foxton Girls

We All Fall Down

The House of Secrets

The Uninvited Guest

Deadly Games

One Last Breath

Still Waters

Vanishing Act

Chill Pill

Bleeding Hearts

The Ghost Portrait

Escape Room

The Final Course

THE FINAL COURSE

Published worldwide by A.W.E. Publishing.

This edition published in 2025

Cover design by Kate Smith

Edited by GS & LW

THE FINAL COURSE

AN O'MALLEY & SWIFT NOVEL
BOOK 14

K.T. GALLOWAY

The food is to die for...

At Blackthorn Hall, the charity gala dinner is the social event of the season. An opulent evening of candle-lit tables, vintage wine, and a menu talked about for weeks. O'Malley and Swift are there to represent the local force, but when a prominent guest vanishes before dessert is served, the celebration turns into a nightmare.

And it seems everyone has something to hide.

The ambitious charity director, the bored wine heiress, the rival caterer desperate to ruin the evening's star chef. As a storm closes in over the Norfolk countryside and the roads become impassable, no one can leave the Hall and no one can be trusted.

Trapped alongside the suspects, O'Malley and Swift must think fast, calling their team to help from afar as the glittering façade of the gala begins to fracture. The truth lurking in the shadows of Blackthorn Hall is far more disturbing than anyone could imagine.

As another guest drops dead, can O'Malley and Swift unmask the killer hiding in plain sight before the final course is served and the last candle gutters out?

Welcome back to the team, dinner is served!

MAILING LIST

Thank you for reading THE FINAL COURSE
(O'Malley & Swift Book Fourteen)

While you're here, why not sign-up to my readers' club where you be the first to hear my news, enter competitions, and read exclusive content:

Join KT Galloway's Reader Club
at ktgallowaybooks.com

FOREWORD

Well, here we are—Book 14!

Annie and Swift are run through the mill, again. I do feel for them sometimes, but it's just so fun seeing how far they're willing to go.

As always, the setting is Norfolk, but the places are all entirely made up.

I really hope you enjoy this twisty, gruesome case —and thank you, as ever, for reading.

Enjoy 😊

ONE

Blackthorn Hall

Lit up from turret to terrace, Blackthorn Hall blazed against the early December evening like the Bat Signal.

Annie O'Malley steered her battered VW up the long drive, headlights sliding over statues that looked half-ready to come alive. Beyond the hall, the last of the daylight was bruising out to grey, scuppering any chances of a visible horizon line.

DI Joe Swift whistled under his breath. "This makes a change from fish and chip Friday."

"Sheesh, you're not kidding," O'Malley replied, her stomach giving a nervous twist. "Are you sure your mum and dad can't make it anymore? What about calling in one of your sisters to join you instead? I'd be happy to drop you off here by yourself and head home for a battered sausage if she can make it."

At work, he was Detective Inspector Swift, her boss and her sounding board, the one person who could read her better than she liked. But tonight, in his dark suit and crooked tie, he wasn't her DI. He was just Joe, her partner.

"I bet you would," Swift snorted. "But you can't have a battered sausage without me. Besides, when mum knew she wasn't going to be well enough to make it this evening, there was no way dad was coming without her. And she wanted *you* to have her ticket. I seem to remember her saying that if you're too nervous to meet the family, the least you can do is eat her dinner for her. And I think my sisters are both on a wellness retreat in Ibiza."

She ignored the less than subtle dig. Annie and Joe hadn't been dating for long, and Annie had enough nightmares with her own family to start thinking about getting to know another one just yet.

"Come on, let's go get drunk on the free champagne and we can thank mum later," Swift went on, putting a comforting hand on Annie's thigh and giving it a squeeze. "I promise you it's not going to be full of annoying, rich people. At least, that's what mum told me when she persuaded me to take their place."

The way Swift's face twisted as he gazed out the window made Annie wonder if he had been duped and was just realising it now it was too late to back out. This was Swift's world, not Annie's. Advertised as a gala dinner and ball to raise money for a charity, but underneath it was just a way for the incredibly rich people in the upper echelons of society to shout about how much they were worth. Great way to raise money, though, pitting their egos against each other in the name of stray cats or wonky donkeys or whatever unfortunate soul this evening's gala was for.

She sighed quietly at the thought, and pulled the car around, following the signs to the front of Blackthorn Hall where she stopped to marvel at the sight. Even if inside was going to be filled with hot air and pretence, at least the outside was easy on the eye. Every window glowed gold and flags of light spilled down to the gravel below. Blackthorn Hall was like the castle in all her childhood fairy tale books. She just hoped it wasn't full of witches and ogres too.

A man in a sharp black coat appeared at her door before she could move on to park up. He opened it with a crisp smile, hand outstretched. Annie blinked, startled. For one hot, mortifying second she thought she was about to get mugged and have her trusty, if somewhat rusty, VW stolen, and she froze, clutching the wheel.

"Er, sorry, can I help you?" she said, kicking herself too late for being polite to a would-be thief.

The man smiled politely. "Valet, ma'am. I can park your car for you."

"Oh." She winced. "Of course. Yes. Obviously. Thank you."

She switched off the engine and handed over the keys, turning to see Swift grinning at her from the passenger seat.

"Not a word," she warned, stepping out in what she hoped was a graceful fashion but almost taking the door off its hinges as she went.

Swift walked around the back of the car, biting his lip. "Who me? Wouldn't dream of it, O'Malley."

He held out his arm and Annie took it, relishing the warmth from his body, despite feeling like her own cheeks were ablaze enough to boil a kettle. It was a clear, crisp night where the lack of cloud cover made the freezing temperatures feel a couple of degrees cooler.

An evening that didn't even nod to the warnings from local weather reports about an incoming storm. There was no way they were in for gale force winds and hail, not when the stars were so bright above them. Annie had secretly been hoping that the weather would arrive in time to trap them at home, well at Swift's, so they could stick with fish and chip Friday and the latest episode of Slow Horses, but the gods had not been in her favour.

Instead, Annie had squeezed herself into a red wine-coloured Gucci dress she'd got for a steal on Vinted. It clashed with her hair, but beggars could not be choosers. Luckily, the dress was so long she could get away with an old pair of golden kitten heels she'd had for longer than she cared to remember and only the shiny toes poked out from underneath. That way, the rich wouldn't be able to tell they were from Primark. Hopefully.

Curling her toes in her shoes to hold them on, Annie walked up the stone steps and entered the hall, her arm still gripped tightly in Swift's. Inside, warmth swallowed them whole. The entrance hall smelled Christmassy, like nutmeg and cinnamon. A waiter with a tightly tied bow-tie appeared out of nowhere and slid Annie's jacket from her shoulders, giving Swift a curt nod.

"Good evening, Detective Inspector Swift, Lady Agatha will be delighted you made it," he said. "We're sorry that Lady Swift was unwell, please do send her our regards."

Lady Swift? Annie barely had time to register the title before the butler disappeared.

"Hi, I'm Annie, nice to meet you!" she laughed. "Do we only get acknowledged if we come with a peerage?"

"And solid gold cufflinks, too," Swift joked, shrugging his shoulders. "Sorry, it's just how we roll."

O'Malley nudged him and took his lead into the depths of Blackthorn Hall making a mental note to talk about his mum's peerage when they weren't surrounded by them. Doors to what looked like a ballroom stood open, spilling out light and laughter. At the far end of the room a quartet played a tune that Annie recognised from Bridgerton. Round tables glittered under chandeliers and champagne glasses caught the light like diamonds. Everything was gilded and gold and Annie felt like she was getting more and more out of her depth.

Swift surveyed the scene. "Whole lot of overdrafts in that room pretending to be philanthropy."

"Shut up and put your nice face on, *Lord* Swift," O'Malley said. "Or your mum will hear of it."

"Urgh, that's my dad, not me. I'm just Joe."

Annie kissed him on the cheek, feeling a graze of stubble beneath her lips.

"Just Joe is perfect for me," she whispered, catching sight of a woman sweeping across the room towards them. "Watch out, you've been spotted."

"Detective Swift, how wonderful you could join us." The woman held out her hand for Swift to take and Annie had to swallow a giggle as he kissed her knuckles. "You must be exhausted after that awful business in the city."

"Occupational hazard," Swift said, putting it mildly. "Lady Agatha, how wonderful to see you again. You look amazing. We appreciate the invite and we're so glad we were able to make it in place of my parents who both send their wishes."

Despite Swift sounding like someone Annie had never met before, he was right, the woman did look incredible in a navy satin dress that looked like it was poured over her body. Her grey hair in a neat up do and her lipstick the perfect shade of pink. Annie would have felt a bit dumpy had it not been for the fact she was too distracted trying to forget the 'awful business in the city' Agatha was referring to.

How Annie and the rest of the Major Crime Unit had been locked in an escape room house by a psychotic ex-inmate they'd put away. They'd nearly paid the price of the ineptitude of the justice system that let the inmate go by mistake. The rest of the MCU had made it out by the skin of their teeth but they were all the more resilient for it.

"And this must be your mother's stand in," Agatha went on, half-smiling in Annie's direction reminding her to suck in her stomach and pull back her shoulders. "We're so grateful for your support. Tonight should be rather special, we've a chef in from London, quite the rising star."

"Good for him," Annie muttered.

Agatha blinked coldly. "You'll adore him. He's carving a name for himself in the most ingenious of ways."

"Lady Agatha," Swift cut in. "Please let me introduce my partner, Annie O'Malley. Annie, this is Lady Agatha Blackthorn, CEO of the Blackthorn charity and host of this wonderful gala party. Agatha, again, thank you for our invite. Mother sends her apologies, she's dreadfully sorry she couldn't make it tonight."

"Of course, dear boy, do send my well wishes back to her." She moved off in a cloud of jasmine before either Annie or Swift could reply.

Swift exhaled. "Oh dear god. Why did I say yes?"

Annie grinned, snagging a champagne flute from a passing tray. "Because your mum guilt-tripped you and promised you free food?"

Swift took another glass and clinked it against hers. "Got it in one. Though I think I block out how bloody awful these people are. I'm sorry they're making you feel… you know."

"I certainly do," she waved her hand as though swatting away a fly. "I should've worn sequins. Or body armour."

"You look perfect," he said simply, eyes lingering just long enough to make her forget about the once overs people were giving her. "Honestly, you could walk in here wearing your MCU hoodie and they'd still stare. It's because you're gorgeous."

"Wait, we have hoodies, since when?" Annie felt her face warm, but she rolled her eyes to cover it. "And flattery will not get you out of a dance later."

Swift smirked. "Wouldn't dream of it. But if you start waltzing like you drive, I might fake an injury."

She laughed, tension starting to ease from her shoulders. "I'll have you know my driving is perfectly acceptable. Also, please can you stop talking like an extra on Downton Abbey every time someone asks you a question. It's unnerving me."

"Sadly not, that's my real voice. I only put on the work one so people will take me seriously back at the station." Swift cleared his throat, brushing his thumb over her knuckles. "Come on, partner. Let's go and get drunk and survive this circus together."

TWO

A RIPPLE OF POLITE APPLAUSE FLUTTERED THROUGH the ballroom as Lady Agatha finished a speech about generosity and how community begins with compassion. Annie was beginning to think that in circles like this, community and compassion were just code for tax write-off.

She drained her champagne and leaned towards Swift. "How many speeches before we get to eat? I'm starving."

Swift smiled into his glass. "At least three."

"Kill me now."

"Not here, O'Malley. You'll ruin the parquet."

Annie laughed quietly, the sound swallowed by the orchestra tuning up for another stately number. The atmosphere inside the ballroom was warm and golden, but Annie was watching through the window at the way the trees were starting to hammer the glass, the wind was beginning to change. Maybe the weatherman had been right after all.

A waiter slipped past with another tray of drinks, and Annie snagged a flute.

“Do you think it’s real champagne or just the Tesco stuff in disguise?”

Swift leaned closer, eyes glinting. “O’Malley, these people wouldn’t know Tesco if it parked on their driveway. Trust me, I grew up with half of them.”

She gave him a look. “Ah yes, every little helps is obsolete here.”

Before he could retort, a voice behind them cut in, warm and amused.

“Still fighting the class war, Joe?”

Swift turned, and his grin was immediate and genuine, something Annie hadn’t seen since they’d arrived.

“Noah bloody Hartwell. You’ve got to be kidding me.” He pulled the man in for a hug and they slapped each other’s backs with their free hands.

Annie thought that the man looked about Swift’s age, maybe a touch younger. He was tall, broad-shouldered, and almost disarmingly ordinary in a room full of polished people. His woollen outer jacket had a light dusting of what looked like cat hair, and his satchel spoke of hard work and not a heaving bank account. Yet he still had the easy confidence of someone who knew which fork to use.

"Didn't expect to see you here," Swift said, breaking out of the hug but clutching the man's hand in his own. "Thought you'd escaped this circus."

"So very nearly," Noah said with a grin. "But I'm doing a bit of work for Agatha so I figured I'd better show up and look grateful."

"Always wise," Swift said, turning to Annie. "Noah this is my partner, Annie. Annie, this is Noah. We grew up a few villages apart and used to cause all sorts of chaos when we were kids."

"He's being kind," Noah added. "My dad ran the stables on Joe's family estate." He freed his hand from Swift's and leant in to Annie and dropped his voice to a whisper. "I'm not one of the upper echelons."

"Me neither," Annie told him. "I'm worried they'll chase me out of the hall with pitchforks if I use the wrong fork for my oysters."

"A girl after my own heart." Noah smiled, sweetly. "But don't let them hear you saying that, oysters don't require a fork. It's just a slurp and a swallow. I can show you how if you'd like me to?"

He winked at Annie and she grinned.

"Christ, Noah," Swift stepped closer and draped an arm over Annie's shoulder. "Ease off the pedal a bit, mate."

Noah burst out laughing and held up his hands in defeat. "Oh, by partner I thought you meant work partner, DI Swift. My bad."

Annie laughed, liking him immediately. There was a groundedness to Noah that made the room feel less brittle.

They grabbed some fresh glasses and stood together near one of the enormous windows, the conversation flowing easily. Outside, the sky was ink-dark now, but a constant stream of clouds raced across the moon. What Annie could see of the gardens was immaculate and she'd love to go have a snoop when it wasn't so dark and cold. A branch whipped against the glass hard enough to make Annie jump.

"Storm's picking up," Noah said, glancing out.

"Good job we all came dressed for it," Annie said, eyeing the ballroom full of bare shoulders peeking out from silk and chiffon. "If anyone has to step outside for a cigarette it's death by exposure, for sure."

Swift chuckled just as a flash of lightning lit the glass. For a moment, the reflection of their faces shimmered there, three shocked faces white in the light, before vanishing again. As the wind moaned through the old frame, a low, uneasy feeling prickled the back of Annie's neck.

She rubbed her arms, trying to shake the chill. "Anyone else feeling that?"

Noah's smile dimmed slightly. "It's the ghosts."

"Ghosts?"

"Yeah," Noah nodded. "Blackthorn Hall always did have a way of holding on to things. People included."

Annie frowned. "What do you mean?"

"That depends who you ask," he said lightly, then tipped his head towards the window again. "But then, I don't believe in ghosts. It's probably just a draft from the single glazing."

"Good," Swift said. "We've had enough hauntings this year. I'll be glad to see the back of her to be honest."

Annie and Swift shared a look. A brief, unspoken memory of the escape-room they almost hadn't escaped from. Noah, catching it, gave a small nod of understanding.

"I read about that," he said quietly. "Hell of a thing. Glad you both made it out."

"Thanks, Noah," Swift said. "I feel like I'm still figuring out what 'made it out' actually means."

Annie nudged him lightly with her shoulder, a silent *I'm fine, you're fine, we're moving on.* She smiled at Noah. "So, apart from ignoring ghosts and winding up Swift, what else keeps you busy?"

Noah's mouth quirked. "These days I'm mostly writing. Bit of local history, social stuff, nothing too grand. I've been working on a book about the old estates around here. How they rose, fell, reinvented themselves. Blackthorn Hall is the centre of the book though; some very interesting stories keep popping out of the woodwork."

Swift arched a brow. "Let me guess, that's another reason you were invited this evening? Lady Agatha making sure she stays on your good side."

"Keep tabs on me more like," Noah said, smiling.

"But, yeah, it is a bit weird, they must have had terrible record-keeping, or someone's been creative with the truth."

Annie tilted her head. "Creative how?"

He hesitated, swirling the wine in his glass and looking at something over Annie's shoulder. "Nah, you know what? Ignore me, I'm just being cynical."

Swift gave a low whistle. "But you're standing in their ballroom. Is that wise?"

"Maybe stupid," Noah said lightly. "Depends how good the pudding is."

Annie smiled, but something in the way he said it made her feel uneasy.

Outside, the thunder rolled again, closer this time, shaking the glass in the windowpane. A deep metallic gong sounded from somewhere beyond the door, a single, resonant note that rolled through the chatter and brought the crowd to a polite, anticipatory hush.

"Showtime," Swift muttered, draining what was left of his drink.

Around them, more guests began drifting into the room, all pearls and tuxedos. Annie watched, mesmerised as waiters glided into formation, guiding people with discreet gestures towards the tables.

"Saved by the dinner bell," Noah said with a grin.

Annie snorted. "Every posh house has one. Next thing you'll tell me is there's a moat."

"There *was*," Swift quipped. "We filled it in when people started falling into it after the parties."

"Naturally."

They joined the slow-moving tide of guests towards the tables. At the edge of the crowd, Noah clapped Swift lightly on the shoulder. "Good to see you again, mate. It's been too long."

"You too," Swift said. "Let's catch up properly after all this, yeah?"

"Definitely." Noah hesitated, his easy smile faltering just slightly. "Actually—" He glanced over Annie's shoulder towards the growing line of diners. "Do you mind if I grab you for a quick word before the night's over? Something I wanted to run by you."

"Of course," Swift said, lowering his voice. "Everything all right?"

Annie leaned in under the pretence of fixing her bag strap, trying, unsuccessfully, to hear what Noah had to say. The hum of conversation rose again, swallowing their words. She caught only the tail end and a few choice words that sounded like *not now, you're liable to lose your appetite.*

"Sure," Swift said again, clapping him on the back. "After dinner."

"See you then," Noah said, giving Annie a friendly nod before slipping away into the throng.

Annie frowned as she watched him go. She turned back to Swift, but he was already scanning the room for their table.

"Come on, O'Malley," he said, offering his arm. "Let's find out where the commoners are sitting."

She smirked, linking her arm through his. "Outside in the storm?"

"Exactly."

They wove between the crowded tables, each draped in white linen and glittering with crystal glassware. Annie leaned over to check the tiny gilt name cards.

Baron and Baroness Something,
The Honourable Someone-Or-Other.

Finally, near the far side of the room, she spotted one that read Detective Inspector Joseph Swift. Next to it, in neat looping handwriting, Miss Annie O'Malley. Swift glanced around as they sat down, surveying the room like a man assessing a crime scene.

"Not bad," he said, straightening his cutlery. "We're not at the back. That's a good sign."

Annie followed his gaze towards the far end of the hall, where a handful of tables sat half in shadow near the band. "You mean with the peasants? We dodged a bullet there"

Annie bit back a laugh as her eyes landed on their table mates, a very elderly man whose white wig had slipped so far askew it looked like it was trying to escape. Next to him, a woman with bright coral lipstick and a martini in each hand was swaying in time with the quartet, mouthing the wrong words.

Swift leaned closer. "Don't speak too soon, we're

with Lord and Lady Fanshawe. Last time I saw her, she tried to auction off her husband."

"Sounds about right," Annie said. "She seems fun."

They shared a grin, before Annie's eyes drifted back across the room over the sweep of white tablecloths and flickering candlelight, all the way up to the head table.

"Hang on," she said quietly. "Is that—?"

Swift followed her line of sight to where Noah sat among the upper echelon, his dark curls an island of normality amid the lacquered heads and jewel-toned gowns. He was leaning slightly away from Lady Agatha, smiling politely as she gestured animatedly with one hand, a flash of diamonds catching the light.

"Huh," Swift said. "Apparently he's been upgraded to dinner guest of honour."

"Or dinner guest under surveillance," Annie muttered.

Swift arched an eyebrow. "Meaning?"

"Meaning," she said, eyes still on the head table, "Lady Agatha doesn't strike me as the type who enjoys the casual company of someone without a title. If she's keeping him that close, she's watching him for a reason."

The storm rattled another window, loud enough to make one of the candelabras tremble. Swift reached for the wine bottle and poured them both a glass.

"Yeah," he said lightly, his forehead crinkling.

"I'll talk to him after supper and make sure he's okay."

Annie smiled, but she couldn't shake the unease curling low in her stomach as she glanced again towards the top table. Noah was laughing at something Lady Agatha said. But the smile didn't reach anywhere near his eyes.

THREE

ANNIE HAD HALF EXPECTED A SOLEMN HUSH TO FALL over the dining room as the hors d'oeuvres arrived. She figured at this level of posh, the only way to dine was in silence, savouring the food with little nods of appreciation and the occasional hum of deliciousness. But she was sorely mistaken.

The moment the waiters withdrew, conversation burst back to life like a fizzy drink, a dozen posh accents tripping over one another in a competition to sound the most interesting. Swift topped up their glasses and glanced around their table.

"I was worried that Agatha was going to sit me beside the ex-wife," he murmured. "But thankfully I can't see her here at all."

"Ha!" Annie choked on her champagne as she tried, and failed, to hold in her laughter. "Imagine that. Would Lady Agatha do that? I thought she liked your family."

Swift gave her a look. “She also loves the Quintons.”

“Oh, that explains the ice queen behaviour. Does Agatha think I stole you away from Sophia? Does she not know about Keith the farmer?”

“Kenneth.” Swift snorted into his napkin.

Annie took a small looking piece of tofu wrapped in something green and as she nibbled on it she felt the stare of Lord Fanshawe sitting next to her and rearranged her face to look posher. She wasn’t sure what that meant but it certainly didn’t involve sniggering like a child into her amuse bouche. He looked to be past retirement age with a thick swathe of white hair that was trying its best to cover a bare pate; his waistcoat reminded Annie of the green wallpaper in Swift’s bedroom. The woman next to him, Lady Fanshawe, kept her own silver-white hair cropped stylishly short and had the air of someone who loved her husband very much, but often found herself cringing at what came out his mouth.

The woman broke into a wide smile. “Ah, new blood! How marvellous. I’m Bea, this is my husband, Colin.”

Colin raised his glass. “Detective Swift now isn’t it? The hero of the hour.”

Swift groaned good-naturedly. “It’s not as glamorous as the papers make it sound.”

“Nothing ever is,” Bea said. “I worked in television once. Everything’s a little smoke and a lot of mirrors.”

Colin chuckled. "Bea produced *Gardener's World* for twenty years, so she knows all about burying things. If I ever go missing, make sure to check under the roses."

"Colin!" she hissed, then laughed herself. "Ignore him, dear. He thinks he's hilarious."

"I am hilarious," Colin said, turning to Annie. "And who might you be? Surely not Lady Swift, if you are then I want the number of your surgeon."

Annie giggled again as Bea swiped her husband's arm with the back of her hand.

"Good lord, Colin, do give over."

Annie could see Swift shaking in his seat, quite obviously trying not to laugh.

"This is Annie O'Malley, my partner in life, and in crime." He managed to compose himself enough to say.

"Hi," Annie lifted her hand in a small wave. "Nice to meet you all."

"Our son, Herb, was supposed to join us, but he was tied up in paperwork. About to move into a place like this and he's busy sorting." Bea fussed with her napkin, pride glowing on her face. "You'd like him though, I'm sure. Well, welcome."

Colin and Bea gave her large smiles back. The table was made up with two other people. One was a young woman, early thirties maybe, wearing a dress that shimmered from silver to pale green as she moved. Her dark hair was slicked back into a low knot and she looked like she'd rather be anywhere else. Beside her, a man in a slightly too-tight tuxedo tapped restlessly at his phone. Neither of them made a move to welcome Annie or Swift.

Annie couldn't work out if they were a couple who hated each other or strangers, she leaned forward, flashing a smile she usually saved for coaxing witnesses into talking.

"So," she said, breaking the silence that had been brewing across the table. "How did you two meet?"

The man looked up sharply, caught off guard. The woman's mouth twitched, almost a smile, before she reached for her wine and sipped.

"We're not together," the man said. "Just seated side by side."

"Ah," Annie said, then sat back, hoping now she'd broken the ice, they'd fill in the rest of the gaps.

"I'm Cassandra," the young woman said finally, her voice as smooth as the silken tablecloth. "Cassandra Blackthorn."

Swift's fork clattered faintly against his plate. "As in—"

"Yes," she said flatly. "As in Lady Agatha Blackthorn. My mother."

"All the way back here?" Annie said, eyebrows lifting.

"That explains the dour face," Bea added cheerfully. "You poor thing. Family gatherings are the worst. Everyone wants to talk about themselves, and you already know how dull they are."

Cassandra's lips twitched again, this time with reluctant amusement. "Something like that."

Swift gave an awkward cough, recovering his composure. "Gosh, sorry Cassie, I didn't recognise you. You were what, thirteen, last time I saw you?"

"Fourteen," Cassandra said. "You came for a charity polo match and broke your wrist falling off the horse."

"Ah. Yes." Swift cleared his throat. "The memory is flooding back. How are you keeping?"

Cassie looked over at the table where her mother was talking the ears of Noah and sighed.

"Oh I'm ticketyboo," she replied, quite obviously not. "Though I am soon to be married, much to my mother's horror, so that's something."

"And you?" Annie asked, turning to the man beside her. "The despised husband-to-be? Bodyguard? Long-lost nephew?"

The man gave a short laugh, surprised into honesty. "I'm Theo Morton. Caterer."

Bea perked up. "Oh! The food is yours? Well I have to say this pork belly wrap is to die for."

"Pork belly?" Annie whispered to Swift, looking at her own tofu. "How come I don't have pork belly? Is it because I'm poor?"

"It's because Mum is pescatarian and she ordered us both the meatless meals with the exception of the fish course." Swift whispered back, lifting his own wrapped tofu.

Theo's smile faltered. "Actually, no, it's not mine. It was supposed to be. My team was booked for the gala months ago, but we were replaced at the last minute. Some 'rising star from London' was brought in instead." He speared the last trace of his starter a little too forcefully. "A guy called Soren Vale. Apparently, he's the new darling of the capital."

"Ah," Colin said, nodding sagely. "The scandal thickens."

"I almost didn't come," Theo admitted. "Didn't fancy watching someone else take the spotlight on my menu. But Agatha insisted. Said it was all in good spirit." He gave a mirthless laugh. "And turning her down tends to be bad for business as they do hire me a lot."

"Sounds like your boss is everyone's boss tonight," Annie said, glancing towards the top table.

Cassie followed her gaze, eyes narrowing faintly. "Don't remind me."

Bea topped up everyone's wine. "Darling, if we're going to talk about the catering industry, I'll need a bigger glass."

Annie laughed, but she caught Theo's expression tightening around the edges. A man quietly nursing resentment. A daughter sitting far from her mother, trying to feign indifference. A storm rising outside. She wondered if it might be shaping up to be one hell of a dinner party.

As if on cue, the waiters swept back in, their

movements perfectly choreographed. Their empty plates vanished and within seconds, new waiters appeared carrying steaming bowls of pale green soup.

Annie blinked. "Efficient, aren't they?"

Theo gave a thin smile but didn't comment. Cassie didn't look up at all, just stirred her spoon absently through the delicate swirl of foam and oil on top. The smell was earthy, leeks, herbs, and something faintly spicy that Annie couldn't quite place. She took a cautious sip and was surprised at the way her taste buds popped to life.

"Delicious," Annie said brightly. "Absolutely delicious."

"Divine," Bea said approvingly, and went back to her own bowl. "Sorry, Theo, should we pretend it's dreadful and send it back to the kitchen."

Theo shook his head, his soup spoon resting at his lips as he too tasted the wares. Annie couldn't help feel sorry for the rejected caterer but the food was too good to be too sorry.

As the chatter around the table resumed, Annie leaned closer to Swift, lowering her voice. "So," she murmured, "what was all that about with Noah earlier? I caught something about losing your appetite, is he okay?"

Swift frowned, absently tracing the rim of his spoon along the edge of the bowl. "I'm not sure. He looked spooked, didn't he? Said he'd talk to me after dinner."

"You think it's about his research on the hall?"

"Maybe," Swift said quietly. "Or something he found while working here. Whatever it was, he didn't want to say it in front of Agatha or her guests."

Annie stirred her soup, pretending to be casual. "You'll check on him after we eat?"

Swift nodded. "Of course."

Outside, the wind picked up again, lashing rain against the tall windows hard enough to make the flames in the candelabras dance. The laughter from the neighbouring tables dimmed slightly as another rumble of thunder rolled overhead.

When Annie looked up from her bowl, Cassie was staring directly at her and she darted her eyes away quickly. She followed Cassie's gaze up the room to the top table where Noah sat next to Agatha, leaning away from her to say something to the man beside him. The man laughed, clapping Noah on the shoulder hard enough to slosh his wine. For a moment, Noah's grin faltered, just slightly, before he pushed back his chair and rose, straightening his jacket.

Annie watched as he slipped between the tables, pausing briefly to exchange polite smiles with a few guests before heading towards the far doors that led out to the corridor. His gait was steady, but his shoulders were tightly set, his jacket taut across them.

She glanced at Swift, catching the flicker of concern in his eyes. He'd seen it too.

"I'll—" he began, half-rising from his chair, but Colin chose that precise moment to lean across the table, waving his wine glass dangerously close to spilling. "So, Joe! Tell us why your lovely mother couldn't be with us this evening? Are her coffers too empty for the charity auction?"

Swift hesitated, torn between politeness and instinct. "Ah, I am sorry to say that she is unwell. And we are as rich as ever."

Colin chuckled. "I'm glad to hear it, old boy. But I am sorry to hear your mother is unwell. Is it something dreadfully grim or is she going to be okay."

Swift laughed politely, the sound just a beat too quick. Annie could see the muscle ticking in his jaw as he tried to keep his focus on their questions.

"Good lord, Colin," Bea said again, rolling her eyes at her husband. "That's private, you can't go asking that kind of question."

Annie leaned back slightly, pretending to sip her wine while keeping her eyes on the far doors. She could hear Swift telling Colin that his mum would be right as rain in a few days but paid no heed as the doors swung silently shut behind Noah.

Cassie was watching too. Their eyes met briefly, a flicker of something like worry flashing and vanishing before Annie could place it. Swift answered another of Colin's enthusiastic questions about his family estate, smiling and nodding like a man on autopilot. Annie knew better. Every line of him was angled towards the exit, towards the friend he was worried about.

He's probably gone for a breather, she thought. Just a breather.

But even as the laughter swelled around her, she couldn't shake the feeling that somewhere in the depths of Blackthorn Hall, the night had already begun to turn.

FOUR

BY THE TIME THE FISH COURSE ARRIVED AND THE first round of the auction was over, Noah still hadn't returned. Annie had only just met the man but she tried not to stare at the doors every thirty seconds. The longer he was gone, the more certain she became that whatever he'd wanted to tell Swift wasn't something mundane. Not that she had any reason to worry, but her spidey senses were tingling and she always listened to them.

Swift had gone quieter too. Normally he could charm his way through any social situation, but now his smile was fixed, and polite, and several shades removed from his real toothy grin.

The fish course was a delicate rectangle of almost translucent flesh rested on a bed of foam so white it looked like shaving cream. Annie poked at it with her fish knife and it fell apart almost immediately.

"Wow," she said, scared to try and lift it in case it slid off her fork and onto the table cloth.

"Cod, apparently," Swift said, checking the menu. "In a lemongrass consommé."

Bea sniffed it suspiciously. "Smells like a spa."

Theo gave a dry smile. "You don't have to make out it's disgusting for my benefit, you know. I can handle competition."

"I wasn't—" Bea began, then sighed. "Oh, fine, I probably was, this is absolutely delicious."

Annie took the leap and dove in, sliding some of the fish and the foam onto her fork. Bea was right, it was absolutely delicious. Unlike anything she'd ever tasted before.

"Don't tell Pete I'm eating foam," she said to Swift, scooping up more onto her fork. "He'd laugh me out of his pizza place and then Sunday would never forgive me."

Annie's flat-cum-office was situated on an old cobbled street in the centre of the city, right above Pete's Pizzas. Sunday, her rescue cat, spent a lot of time down there, mostly hanging out in the warmth when Annie was away on a case, but also pretending to the customers and Pete that he was perpetually starved and needed fattening up. If he got any fatter he wouldn't fit through his cat flap.

A waiter swooped in to refill their glasses with a smile. "Everything to your satisfaction, madam?" he asked.

"Absolutely amazing, thank you so much," she gushed.

He inclined his head and glided away and Annie felt Swift squeeze her hand. She looked up at him and his real smile was back.

"You know that's probably the nicest feedback he'll get this eve?" Swift told her. "It's normally a polite nod if the food is to die for, or a quirk of the head if it's not positive feedback."

"Was I too much?" she asked, panicking.

"You're never too much," Swift replied, giving her a peck on the nose. "You're you."

Annie grinned into her chest and took a sip of wine. Out of the corner of her eye she saw Cassie watching her. Annie pretended to adjust her napkin, but when she glanced back, Cassie's gaze had already flicked away towards her own plate. Her instincts hummed. Cassie's smile earlier had been brittle, her laughter half a beat late, and now she was watching Swift more than she was eating.

Maybe it was just anxiety. Or maybe it was something else entirely.

Annie tilted her head, studying her for a second longer. Cassie was pretty in a polished, effortless sort of way. But there was something in the way she looked at Swift that prickled under Annie's skin. A look of admiration or nostalgia? Or something more complicated.

She forced herself to look away.

Don't be ridiculous, she told herself. Cassie had

said she's getting married and, more importantly, Swift was hers.

The last traces of the fish course were cleared away and for a few blissful moments the conversation lulled, leaving only the hum of the storm outside and the soft clinking of cutlery being reset.

Annie glanced towards the doors again. Still no sign of Noah. That was two courses he would have missed now. Surely not just a bathroom break or a cigarette stop. Agatha once again rose from her seat and walked to the stage for the second round of auction goodies. The first round had seen the guests bid on Cartier and Mont Blanc, now it was time for the excursions. But there were no go-karting days to be seen, this was all Spa retreats in Bali or Botox. Annie sat on her hands so she didn't accidentally bid on a few fillers and watched in awe as the figures rose.

As the hammer came down on the last item, the wind gave a sudden howl, battering the windows hard enough to make one of the chandeliers tremble. For half a second, the lights flickered. A few guests gasped, laughter bubbling up after like a nervous overture.

"Nothing says fine dining like the threat of electrocution," Bea said dryly.

Colin chuckled. "Adds a certain spice, though."

Before Annie had time to think about how heavy the chandelier above their head might feel if it crashed to their table, the waiters returned in two perfect lines, moving with the smoothness of a stage production. Silver domes gleamed, each set down in unison before being lifted in a single, synchronised flourish.

Annie blinked at her plate.

"Woodland Reverie," Swift read from the card beside his. "Or, in our case, the vegetarian version. Truffled beet and wild mushroom parcel with red wine jus."

"Yummy," Annie said, inhaling the scent.

Bea peered down at her own plate. "Mine's a slab of something that still looks alive."

"Rare," Colin said, delighted. "Look at that colour. Beautiful."

The rich and savoury, faintly metallic smell hit, making Annie's stomach grumble despite herself.

Theo stared at his dish, frowning. "That's not right."

Swift looked up. "What's not?"

Theo gestured with his fork. "The menu listed côte de boeuf. This isn't that. Different cut, different grain entirely."

Bea looked scandalised. "Good heavens, are we being fed supermarket steak?"

Theo gave a small, humourless laugh. "No, not that. It's just unusual. This looks like it hasn't been rested properly. Which is strange at this level."

"Maybe Chef Vale isn't all he's cut out to be," Annie said, trying to sound casual. "Bit of a hack like Salt Bae or whoever that guy was who charged crazy prices for throwing some salt in the direction of his diners."

Theo didn't say anything, he was still prodding the meat as though it might answer for him.

"I'm almost glad mum's veggie," Swift murmured to Annie. "Whatever breed of cow that is, I'm not sure I don't trust it to get up and walk away."

"Lordy," Annie said lightly, though her appetite had dimmed too. "It's probably some experimental farm-to-table thing."

Bea cut into her portion, inspecting the pink centre with approval. "Well, I think it's divine. Tender as sin."

"Can't argue with that," Colin said, already halfway through his. "Who cares what it is as long as it tastes like this?"

Annie forced a smile and took another sip of wine, trying to focus on the laughter bubbling up around the table. Bea was regaling them with a story about filming *Gardener's World* in a thunderstorm and nearly electrocuting Alan Titchmarsh. Even Colin was chuckling so hard he was wheezing.

But under it all, the storm was building harder and faster now. Rain battered the windows in sheets, the sound like applause from an invisible audience. A flash of lightning turned the room momentarily white, and in the afterglow, Annie caught sight of Lady Agatha at the head table, smiling that tight, camera-ready smile as her guests laughed and dined around her.

Only one seat near her remained empty. Noah's. Swift followed Annie's gaze, their eyes meeting briefly. Neither of them spoke, but the same thought moved between them like static.

"Still nothing?" she whispered.

He shook his head. "Maybe he went outside for air, but that was nearly an hour ago. He'd have frozen by now and be soaked to the skin. I'll give it until the next course. Then I'm going to find him."

When the plates were cleared again, Cassie excused herself, murmuring something about the ladies' room. Her chair scraped softly against the floor, and Annie watched her disappear towards the door.

A moment later, Theo followed suit. "Need to make a call," he said quickly. "I'll be back before dessert. Don't eat mine."

Bea leaned towards Annie, whispering conspiratorially. "If they're doing something naughty in the toilets, I'm getting both their puddings. They told us they weren't together."

"Deal," Annie whispered back, though she felt no humour in it. The hairs on her arms had risen without warning. Something about the ebb and flow of people leaving was starting to feel weird.

Cassie returned ten minutes later, composed once more, her sleek hair back in place and her smile restored.

"I hope I haven't missed dessert," she said lightly, slipping back into her chair.

Annie leaned in. "You nearly lost it to Bea, but you're back just in time."

That drew a small laugh around the table, the tension thinning a little. Even Swift managed to relax his shoulders again. A few minutes later, Theo reappeared too, brushing a damp sleeve as he slid into his seat.

"Wi-Fi's dreadful," he muttered. "Couldn't get a signal anywhere."

"Welcome to the countryside," Colin said cheerfully. "No signal, no Uber, and the horses are more expensive than the cars."

That earned a ripple of laughter, and from there the evening settled into something almost normal. The main course plates were cleared and desserts arrived in the form of miniature works of art that Annie devoured with gleeful abandon.

By the time the last of the auction rounds began, the wine had done its work. Annie found herself actually enjoying the soft hum of conversation and the ridiculous bidding wars that had way too many digits to add up. When the final hammer fell and the last round of applause faded, the crowd began to thin. Guests drifted towards the exits, clutching coats and draining their glasses. The ballroom emptied almost as quickly as the pockets of the bidders.

"See?" Bea said, rising carefully from her chair and straightening her wrap. "Told you it'd be fun. You survived posh soup, posh meat, and posh philanthropy. You should absolutely take that as a win."

Before Annie could reply, a soft voice cut through the chatter. "Detective Swift, Miss O'Malley, I do hope you're not sneaking off just yet."

Lady Agatha was gliding towards their table, her gown catching the light as she moved. Her expression was all charm, but there was a faint glint in her eyes that suggested she didn't often hear the word *no.*

Swift stood politely, smoothing down his jacket. "Of course not, Lady Agatha. Thank you again for having us."

"Don't thank me just yet," she said. "You must join me for a nightcap in the drawing room before you brave that storm. It's a dreadful mess out there, and I insist on sending you off with something warming in your bellies." Agatha's gaze swept across the table.

"And of course it would be rude of you not to invite their delightful dinner companions, too" Colin piped up, clearly thinking of the brandy.

Bea's face lit up. "I never say no to a drink I don't have to pour myself."

Cassie gave a tight smile, but nodded all the same. "Of course, Mother. How could we possibly refuse?"

Theo nodded silently, looking at his half-finished glass of wine.

"Well, looks like I don't have a say in the matter," Agatha said, flatly. "The staff have a fire going already. This way, everyone."

She turned, her presence carrying the group in her wake like a tide. Annie caught Swift's eye as they followed.

“I get the impression we couldn’t have left then even if we wanted to?” she murmured.

Swift gave a low laugh. “Nope.”

They followed Agatha down the hallway, their footsteps muffled by the growing growl of the storm outside. The whole place felt quieter now. From what Annie could see, most of the guests had already gone, probably fleeing before the storm hit so badly they were trapped. Most of the staff had left too.

A thunderclap cracked overhead, loud enough to shake the windowpanes. And then the lights went out and everything vanished in a single, suffocating instant. Someone gasped and a glass shattered against the floor. The darkness was total, pressing close on all sides.

“Everyone stay calm,” Lady Agatha’s voice commanded from somewhere ahead, smooth and unflappable even now. “It’s probably the storm taking out the electrics. These old houses—”

Her voice faltered.

Annie couldn’t see her own hand in front of her face. Couldn’t see Swift, though she felt the whisper of his arm brushing hers. Then his fingers found her wrist and shuffled down until they were wrapped in her own.

“Just a blip,” he murmured.

The wind roared outside, rattling the windows so hard she thought they’d shatter.

And then silence as Blackthorn Hall and all the remaining occupants held their breath.

FIVE

For a suspended second after the lights went out, nobody moved.

Bea's breath hitched sharply beside her, at least Annie thought it was Bea's. Behind that was the gentle scrape and clink of someone feeling around with their shoe for the fallen glass.

Annie thought you could learn a lot about a person by how they reacted in an emergency. Whoever it was trying to tidy away the broken crockery was a people person, caring enough to not want others to get hurt by the sharp shards. She did also notice that while Swift's hand tightened around hers, there was no noise whatsoever from Cassie or Theo who had left the room first.

Lady Agatha, however, spoke like a woman who was quite happy to take on the ghastly weather and the way it had taken out her electrics, and win.

“Not to worry,” she sang. “Happens all the time. Nobody move.”

It was a comforting lie, and Annie knew it, but she kept still all the same.

“Peter, Alice, fetch some candles,” she commanded to an unseen force. “Quickly, now.”

A door thudded open and footsteps hurried in their general direction. Outside, the wind roared harder. When the first flame sparked to life, it was a small, quivering circle in a sea of black. Then another, and another, until faces flickered back into being, pale and startled in the sudden gold light.

A young man dressed in the classic black and white of the staff stood holding a candelabra that trembled faintly in his hands.

“Your drawing room, my lady?” he asked.

“Yes,” Agatha said, and the single syllable clicked the group back into motion.

They set off down the corridor in a cautious procession, the light from the candles lifting and falling like fireflies. Their shadows rippled across the walls, huge and distorted. Every few steps, lightning flashed through the tall windows, flooding the hall with stark white light before plunging them back into the soft gold.

“Remind me to write a strongly worded letter to the National Grid,” Colin muttered. “Dear Sirs, please stop terrifying my wife.”

“Dear Colin,” Bea whispered. “Please stop talking.”

Swift gave a quiet huff of laughter. "All right?" he asked, his voice low near Annie's ear.

"All good, thanks," she whispered back, though her heart was pounding. "You?"

"Can't complain."

They both sniggered into the dark as they knew that complaining was one of Swift's favourite past times.

The butler with the candles opened a door ahead and a rush of firelight covered the hallway. He ushered them through into the drawing room and darted away again just as they took a collective breath. Even in just the firelight it was magnificent, floor-to-ceiling bookshelves, heavy curtains, a rug that looked as though it needed its own postcode. And most importantly, the fire crackling in the hearth, throwing out enough heat to make Annie's skin prickle.

"Do sit," Agatha said, gesturing to the large sofas and upright armchairs dotted around the fire.

The guests settled happily. Bea and Colin claimed one of the sofas. While Theo took the other. Cassie drifted to the window, parting the curtain just enough to peer out at the rain, sigh, before she took a seat next to Theo. Swift and Annie were swallowed up by a pair of wingback chairs either side of the large hearth, and Agatha took the remaining armchair opposite the flames. Her face danced with the reflection of the fire, shadows growing and shrinking with the movement. Annie watched as she took a moment, relaxing her face so much that the tiredness sprang out in the way her skin slackened. Seconds later she'd pulled herself back together and was as poised as ever.

"I think a drink is in order." She nodded once and the butler and his female counterpart appeared moments later, bearing more candles, decanters, and glasses which they set upon the table in the centre of the seats.

Annie leant to pour herself and Swift a whisky but she was beaten to it by the young waitress who had seen her move and darted forward to tip a generous glug each into two crystal glasses. She handed them to Annie and Swift and stepped back into the shadows before Annie could thank her. Sipping the most delicious whisky she'd had in a while, Annie saw that the others had drinks too, and none of them had moved. Being rich was like a well-oiled machine run by AI, it seemed quite fun to start with but she was sure brain rot would soon set in if she had nothing to do.

"I apologise for the disruption," Agatha said. "They'll have the generator going shortly."

"Do they pedal it?" Bea asked, sipping her brandy.

Annie laughed softly, but Swift didn't. His gaze had shifted towards the now closed door; his expression was tight. If Annie had to guess, she'd hazard that he was thinking of Noah.

The wind clawed at the windows, and somewhere

outside them something banged and crashed at the hall.

Swift took out his phone and stared at the blank screen. "I was going to call mum and see how she is, but I don't have any reception or Wi-Fi. You?"

Annie scrambled for her small cross body bag, glad that she hadn't taken it off, and pulled out her phone.

"No signal or Wi-Fi either, sorry." She knew Swift didn't really want to check on his mum, no matter how much he loved and cared about her, his insistence wasn't about her. Annie wondered what was going on in his head.

He looked towards Agatha. "Do you have a landline, Agatha? I just wanted to check in on Mother."

"Down, I'm afraid," she said. "A tree took out the line earlier. I'm sure she's fine, though, she's with Lord Swift too, right?

Swift nodded.

"Good," Agatha went on. "In which case we'll sit by the fire and talk to one another, it's frightfully wholesome."

Colin groaned. "God forbid."

"Cassie, why don't you start by telling everyone what your plans are for New Year's Eve?" Agatha spat. "We'll see if everyone else thinks your choices are as laughable as I do."

"Mother."

"Though a wedding might solve a few of our problems."

"Where's your generator?" Theo interrupted, looking at the way Cassie was curled so tightly in on herself she was barely noticeable on the sofa. "Basement?"

Agatha's smile didn't reach her eyes. "It's being attended to. You needn't concern yourself."

"I'm happy to help," he said, voice drowned out by the boom of thunder at the window.

Cassie flinched and crossed her legs tightly underneath her, eyes on the thick curtains at the window.

"No." Agatha wasn't to be budged.

"To conversation, then." Theo lifted his glass. Though he looked like the last thing he wanted to engage in was conversation with the very woman who had sacked him off for another chef last minute.

Swift must have seen that Theo was about to say something of the sort and he jumped in first with his own question.

"Lady Agatha, would it be okay if I went to check on a friend? He left during dinner and never returned and I'd love to catch up with him if he's still here."

Agatha turned, every inch the hostess. "Detective, I must insist that no one wanders the house during the storm and the power cut. The corridors are dark, the floors uneven and I don't want any accidents on my watch."

"With respect," Swift said, "I've been through worse."

Agatha's smile didn't change, but her eyes cooled. "And I've hosted worse, Joseph. Please sit down."

"Well perhaps you could tell me what happened to him, then?" Swift sat with a thump but was undeterred. "Noah Hartwell, he was sitting next to you, currently writing a book about the estate and the family as I gather. We were good friends as children and wanted to catch up properly after the auction."

"Ah yes, he left as he was feeling unwell, perhaps you can catch up at another time?"

The silence that followed was thick enough to feel. Annie could almost hear Swift's cogs turning and she was right there with him. Noah wouldn't have left without saying goodbye, would he?

Bea topped up her glass, offering the bottle to everyone else who shook their heads.

"We're all friends here," she said brightly, though her voice cracked a little. "Anyone up for a game of charades?"

No one answered. Not even the mother and daughter could break the tension in the room. In fact, Agatha was doing her best to keep it strung taut, from what Annie could work out. She just wasn't sure why. Agatha had asked Annie and Swift to join her for a night cap, yes the rest of the table might have invited themselves too, but why wasn't she talking? Was she more worried about the storm and the electrics than she was letting on?

Another few awkward minutes ticked past as the storm raged and the fire crackled. Every sound felt magnified, the creak of floorboards, the whisper of fabric as someone shifted in their chair, even the tick of the mantel clock seemed too loud.

It was only when the butler and maid returned, that Annie realised how tense her shoulders had been and she shrugged them out. Both staff members looked pale and slightly damp around the edges. The butler leant down to whisper something to Lady Agatha; as he straightened Annie caught the pinch on Agatha's face.

"We're heading down to the cellar," the butler reported, loudly. "To check the generator."

He hesitated.

Agatha's voice sliced cleanly through the pause. "Thank you, Peter, Alice. That will do."

He nodded and started to back away, the maid following like his shadow. Annie's pulse gave an uncomfortable kick. But Bea broke the air as she shuffled out of her seat and offered Colin a hand up after her.

"I'm so sorry to be a pest," she said. "But I must visit the lady's room. Colin here will come with me to make sure I'm okay. But please could we borrow a candle to light our way?"

"You should have asked one of the staff before they left for the cellar," Agatha replied, face hardened. "But if you must go then please do be careful. Don't get lost or go in any rooms other than the powder room and come right back."

Annie grimaced, she felt like she was at primary school and her fellow pupils were being told how to take their bathroom breaks. Colin gave a salute and the two left the room, closing the door behind them.

They once again descended into silence. The fire crackling on top of one too many champagnes was making Annie feel tired. She wished Agatha would hurry up and tell them why she'd invited them to stay for a nightcap so she could go home and get into bed.

Agatha put down her glass and lent forward, steepling her hands. It looked like she was finally ready to talk when a sound burst through the silence.

At first it blended with the wind in a high, distant thread. Then it grew clearer, and unmistakable.

It was a scream.

It was raw and terrible, the kind pulled from somewhere deep inside. It sliced through the storm, rose, and broke apart. Annie felt her scalp crawl with the sound, like insects pulling at her hair. For a beat, no one moved and Annie watched them. Cassie froze mid-turn, eyes wide and gleaming. Theo's mouth tightened into a single word that didn't make it out past his lips. Agatha stood very slowly, the brandy in her glass perfectly level.

"Everyone, stay where you are," she told them.

Agatha walked with grace but Annie could tell she wanted to move as quickly as possible. As soon as she shut the door behind her, Swift was already on his feet. Annie rose with him.

"Annie," he said.

"On it." Her voice was steady, even if her hands

weren't. What if it had been Bea, what if she'd fallen and hurt herself?

Theo and Cassie gaped at Annie and Swift as they snuck across the room to the door. Swift pulled it open a notch and peered out.

"Stay here," he told them, then whispered to Annie, "with me." and they slipped out into the corridor. Outside, the wind clawed at the house as the echoes of the scream faded into the storm.

SIX

PETER, THE YOUNG BUTLER, STOOD FROZEN A FEW paces outside the door, a candle shaking in his grip making the shadow of the flame dart across the walls. Alice looked as though she'd rather melt into the wallpaper than head further into the darkened corridors. But Agatha was nowhere to be seen.

Annie and Swift walked up to the staff; with no lights themselves they needed support and Annie was just glad it was these two to provide it and not the lady of the house. Though she had thought these two were down in the cellar trying to fix the generator.

"Where did the scream come from?" Swift asked.

"Near the cellar doors," Peter replied, biting the inside of his cheek so hard his cheekbones cut into his skin. "We ran back when we heard it."

"All right. Show us."

Alice looked horrified but Annie knew Swift wasn't messing around and she gave the young girl a friendly smile. The look she gave Annie back was less than friendly, but Alice and Peter set off anyway. Annie fell in step beside them, her dress brushing the polished floorboards. The candlelight trembled over the walls, catching on gilt frames and ghostly portraits whose eyes seemed to follow them down the corridor.

The storm's rumble had settled into a low, steady growl and a sound cracked through the dark behind them. A sharp click and then the unmistakable creak of a door easing open. Annie spun round, her heart hammering painfully in her chest. Quick, light footsteps, padded over the parquet towards them. A hand caught her arm. She yelped, jerking back before her brain caught up to the face in front of hers.

"Jesus, Theo!" she hissed.

Theo raised both hands, the candlelight carving hollows under his eyes.

"Easy, sorry. Didn't mean to make you jump."

Swift turned, frowning. "Why are you following us?"

"I'm coming too."

"I told you to stay where you were." Swift's face darkened.

Theo shrugged. "And yet here I am."

Swift muttered swear words under his breath but he gestured for the staff to continue on their journey to the source of the scream. Fine by Annie. If Theo had done something, he was the type to trip himself up soon enough.

A door funnelled them deeper into the back of the

hall. The air grew colder, carrying a damp, earthy smell of stone that never quite dries out. Lighting and thunder crashed and flashed almost simultaneously and the maid whimpered under her breath. Annie couldn't blame her. Every gust of wind made the old hall creak. She tried to ignore the tightness in her own chest. There had been plenty of worse places Annie had been stuck in, but this one crawled beneath her skin.

They passed a small, cupboard door and stopped at a larger one as the candle flames bent towards it as if pulled by its breath.

"What's that?" Annie asked.

Peter's knuckles were white around the candelabra. "The cellar, the generator's down there, Miss. Vale went to check it not that long ago."

Theo's eyes flicked to him. "The chef?"

"Yes, sir."

Annie exchanged a glance with Swift. *Why did the chef go and check on the electrics when there is a house full of staff who know the building?*

She didn't like that thought at all. Especially when she paired it with a bloodcurdling scream from this direction.

Swift stepped up and pulled the door wider. The narrow stairwell yawned before them, the stone steps dropping into darkness below. The smell hit them. It rolled out of the cellar like breath from something that had been sleeping for too long. Annie baulked and took a step back, but Swift seemed undeterred.

"Stay here," he told the others.

"Not a chance," Annie said, already stepping onto the first stair.

The others hesitated for only a second before following. It seemed no one wanted to be left alone in the dark, even if the alternative was a stinky cellar. Peter clutched his candelabra in front of him like a shield, but Annie didn't doubt it could do damage if he swung it at someone. The thing was solid silver and looked heavy. She slowed a bit and let him move in front of her, protesting that he knew the place and he had the light, but really it was to give herself a fighting chance if the swamp monsters it smelt like started to rise. Some police officer she was.

The steps were narrow and the deeper they went, the colder it became. Annie's breath began to cloud faintly in front of her face. At the bottom of the stairs was a small chamber lined with wine racks. Dozens of old bottles gleamed dully in the candlelight, their labels so dusty they had turned to illegible ghosts. It was empty of anything other than thousands of pounds worth of squashed grapes.

Peter edged towards a doorway to the left. "Generator room's through here," he said.

Swift nodded. "Let's have a look."

The room beyond was even smaller, little more than a concrete box filled with the dead hulk of the generator. Its metal casing was slick with condensation. A single inspection lamp swung from a hook above it, the bulb blinking feebly as if trying to decide whether to give up hope too.

Swift crouched in front of it, running a hand along the panel. "It's dead. Probably overloaded when the power went."

"Can you fix it?" Theo asked.

"I'm a detective, not an electrician. To be honest I don't even know why I'm kneeling down pretending to know what I'm doing. Peter, Alice, how about you?"

The butler and the maid shook their heads quickly, eyes fixed on the floor.

Annie swept her torch beam slowly around the room. "There's no one down here. No sign of a struggle either. Maybe the scream came from somewhere else?"

Peter exhaled in relief, lowering his candle. "Maybe it was just the storm. Wind in the trees or through the windows, perhaps?"

But Annie wasn't convinced. "Then where's the chef? And where did Lady Agatha go?"

They stood in uneasy silence, listening to the faint hiss of rain against the tiny vent window high in the wall. The wind made the frame moan like a tiny scream itself.

"All right," Swift said finally. "Let's check back upstairs. If Vale came down here, he'd have gone back to the kitchen, right?"

They retraced their steps, the candles sputtering as they climbed. Annie's legs were cold to the bone, her feet like blocks of ice in her stupid shoes. Luckily the kitchen wasn't far away from the cellar entrance and it was warm, but it was also empty.

It was a large room, a set of doors to the outside at the far end were shut tight, though the wind still whistled through every gap it could find. Every surface gleamed and looked to be scrubbed within an inch of its life. A few pans sat drying by the sink, their polished copper undersides catching the candlelight. Heat still billowed from the big range but there was no sign of anyone. Not Vale, not even the usual scurrying of staff trying to reset things after a big event like the one they'd laid on that evening.

Swift crossed to the prep table in the middle of the room. "You'd think someone would've stayed to mind the place."

"I think most of the staff will have left after clean up, it's a small team really, sir," Peter said.

"More than small," Alice added. She turned to Peter, wide eyed. "We should really be getting to work on the fires; Lady Agatha will not be pleased if she sees us dithering."

"We're hardly dithering, Alice," Peter admonished. "We're helping the police with their investigation."

Annie didn't think it was an investigation, and she hoped it stayed that way. Scream or no scream, she was exhausted and freezing and really wished she'd stayed at home for fish and chip Friday. Something caught her eye as she headed around the kitchen to stand next to the oven.

Annie frowned. "Joe, look."

Half-hidden behind a stack of empty platters, a leather roll lay sprawled open on the counter. Its contents glinted faintly.

Swift moved closer, his face tightening. "Looks like a chef's knife kit. Pretty normal for a kitchen the size of this one, and for a chef who's been brought in from London."

Theo snorted from the doorway. "Chefs from Norfolk have knife kits too, you know."

Annie ignored him and reached out, gingerly touching the edge of one of the handles. The knives were arranged neatly, each in its slot, except the largest carving knife, which was missing entirely. The leather itself was dark and tacky under her fingers.

"Blood," she said softly.

Theo shifted, folding his arms. "It's a chef's knife, Annie. Meat was served. There'll be blood. Not everything has to be tied up in murder and foul play, you know."

He seemed be trying for a casual tone, but it didn't land right. His voice was too loud for the hush that had settled over the kitchen, and it bounced off the tiled walls like a stray bullet.

Annie didn't answer straight away. She looked around the room instead. Every surface gleamed. The counters, the chopping boards, even the metal ladles hanging by the range had been polished within an inch of their lives. The kind of sterile shine that only came from using a shit tonne of elbow grease. Her stomach gave a slow, uneasy twist.

"Then why is everything else so spotless?" she said quietly.

Theo opened his mouth, but no sound came out. The candlelight caught the sweat beading along his temple. Before anyone could say another word, another scream ripped through the silence.

But this wasn't the distant, echoing kind they'd heard before. This scream sounded like it was right outside the external kitchen doors. It was sharp and raw, bouncing off the walls, cutting through the air so violently that Annie's whole body flinched. Peter dropped his candle, splattering wax across the floor as the room was plunged into blackness. He swore loudly, breaking character from the stiff upper lip he'd been forcing. Annie heard him sweep his hands across the floor and then strike a match, illuminating the space around him like a halo. It wasn't long before he had relit the candle.

For a heartbeat, no one moved. No one dared to open the doors and face what had happened.

Annie reached for Swift's arm, her fingers trembling despite herself.

"Joe," she whispered. "Please tell me that was the wind."

He didn't answer. His jaw was set, eyes locked on the heavy door, and then he pulled it open.

SEVEN

A GUST OF FREEZING AIR TORE THROUGH THE kitchen, snuffing the candle Peter had just lit. Annie had a flash of inspiration at the shouts that followed and kicked herself for not thinking of it earlier. She drew out her phone, which still had no connection, and turned on the torch.

"Oh, yeah," Theo said, blinking in the sudden beam. "Forgot that would work."

"Good lord," Peter muttered, fumbling for his own phone "I didn't even think—"

"Me neither," Annie admitted. "Feels like the house hypnotised us into thinking we'd gone full Victorian."

A few more phones lit up around the kitchen, harsh LED light chasing the darkness back into the corners.

"Guess we're not completely powerless after all," Swift said wryly, his face half in shadow.

"Speak for yourself," Alice's voice floated in from the doorway, brittle with tension. "My battery's on one percent."

Even through the fear, Annie smiled faintly. It was absurd to be standing in a centuries-old hall, surrounded by candelabras and marble busts, yet holding up rectangles of light like urban explorers. Still, it was a comfort, however fragile, to have that cold, artificial glow piercing the dark.

Footsteps pounded towards them and out of the dark, a figure stumbled into view. It was Cassie Blackthorn. Her hair was loose, wet from the rain, and her mascara had smudged down her cheeks.

"There's—" she gasped, pointing over her shoulder, her voice cracking. "There's someone—"

Swift caught her by the arms before she could fall. "Cassie, slow down. What's going on, why are you outside?"

"Chef Vale," she managed. "He's—he's—"

The rest was lost in a fresh crash of thunder. Swift handed her gently to Alice and shone his phone torch in Peter's direction. "With me."

Cassie shook her head violently. "Don't, please, don't go out there. It's horrible."

But Swift was already gone. Annie swallowed hard, and followed, heart thudding as she pushed through the door into the raging storm.

Rain slashed sideways across the lawn, cold needles biting at her skin. Her heels sank into the sodden grass with every step. Swift's phone beam carved a narrow path through the downpour, Peter not too far behind him, catching flashes of silver on the wet ground ahead.

"Joe?" she called, but the wind swallowed her voice whole.

Annie's torchlight swept over the churned grass and the faint, glistening trail that led away from the kitchen door. A few steps further and she saw the dark stains on the lawn washed thin by the rain. And then came the shape.

"Swift," she started, but he'd already seen it.

Who Annie guessed was the Chef, Soren Vale, lay sprawled on the lawn, face up, one arm twisted awkwardly beneath him. His white jacket had turned a deep, spreading red that the rain couldn't quite rinse away. The blood pooling around him was already seeping into the grass, streaking away in small rivulets.

Annie dropped to her knees next to the chef. The shock of the cold water soaked through her skirt, but she didn't care. She pressed two fingers to the side of his neck, searching for a pulse but she already knew she wouldn't find it.

Swift crouched opposite her, rain running down his face. "Annie?" he said quietly.

She shook her head at him and dropped her hand, the feeling hitting like a punch. The wind roared and a fork of lightning split the sky, throwing the entire garden into harsh, white light. In that second, she saw everything in perfect clarity. Vale's open eyes, the numerous slashes across his white coat, their edges stained red.

Peter stumbled forward, his voice trembling. "Oh God, oh God."

Swift rose, scanning the garden. "We need to move him inside before all the evidence is washed away."

Annie forced herself upright, her legs shaky and her heart rattling painfully against her ribs. The last thing she wanted to do was carry a dead body across a muddy lawn in kitten heels but she knew they couldn't leave Vale out here. Evidence or not. They owed it to him as a human being to treat him with respect.

Swift slipped his hands beneath the chef's shoulders while Peter took his legs. Annie hesitated for only a heartbeat before scooping her hands under his back and helping him stay relatively horizontal as the men lifted.

Vale wasn't as heavy as Annie had expected him to be, but there was a terrible weight to him all the same. Which wasn't helped by the relentless curtain of rain that soaked them to the bone. Swift's phone torch cut a narrow beam through the downpour, lighting their slow path back towards the kitchen door. The grass squelched underfoot, every step a struggle through mud.

Alice waited in the doorway, one trembling hand clamped over her mouth. "Oh God," she whispered as they reached her. "Poor guy, what happened to him?"

"Clear a space," Swift said gently. "Let's get him in and set him down."

Annie's arms were aching by the time they eased Vale's body down onto the floor. The warmth of the kitchen felt wrong now and steam rose faintly from the dead man's clothes as the heat began to dry the rain.

"Do you think we should take him down to the cellar?" Annie whispered to Swift as Peter went to fetch some towels.

Swift rubbed a hand over his rain-soaked hair. "It's cold enough down there. Might be best until the police arrive. Can you take some photos of him now, do it quietly, just so we have a record of this?"

Annie nodded, swiping her phone open to the camera app and taking a batch of photos as Theo appeared beside them staring at the dead chef with wide eyes. His gaze flicked from Annie to the body on the floor.

"Jesus," he muttered, stepping closer. "That's Vale. What happened to him?"

Annie expected shock, or grief, or nausea but instead Theo's mouth hardened into a scowl. Swift caught Annie's eye, and she knew they were thinking the same thing. That wasn't how most people looked at the freshly dead, no matter how used to slabs of meat they were. Before she could question him, another set of footsteps clicked sharply against the tiles and Lady Agatha swept in, her presence filling the room as much as her battery-operated torch. Her gown was still immaculate but her hair stuck to her head with dampness.

"What on earth is all this noise?" she demanded, her gaze cutting through them until it landed on Vale's still form. Her face didn't move at first. Then, very slightly, her nostrils flared. "Good Lord."

Swift straightened. "I'm sorry, Lady Agatha, but I'll need to call this in. We'll have to get the police out here immediately."

Agatha blinked, the words seeming to take a moment to reach her. "That won't be possible."

"I'm sorry?" Swift said.

She folded her arms. "The phone lines are still down."

"Then we'll go and get the police," Annie said quickly. "I can drive out until I get a signal. We can—"

Agatha cut across her. "You can't. There's another tree down across the main drive. I've already sent a man to check. No one's getting through."

Annie's stomach dropped. She glanced at Swift, but his jaw was already set. It was too far to walk to the nearest town, especially in the storm, who's to tell how many other trees might fall in the winds?

"What do we do?" Annie asked Swift.

"We wait," Agatha replied, ignoring Swift. "We'll reconvene in the drawing room until this wretched weather passes. There's no sense in standing over him."

"With respect, Lady Agatha," Swift said, "there's

every sense in standing over him, he's all we have left of a crime scene."

Something sharp flickered in Agatha's eyes, gone almost before Annie could name it. "Joseph, this is my home. You'll do me the courtesy of treating it as such."

Annie held her breath, waiting for the explosion, but Swift only nodded tightly. "Fine. Peter and I will move Mr Vale down to the cellar for now. He'll need to be kept somewhere out of the way until the authorities can reach us."

Agatha inclined her head, already turning towards the door. "Do as you see fit. The rest of us will go back to the fire. You must all be freezing."

It wasn't a suggestion. Annie lingered, watching as Swift and Peter squatted down beside Vale's body, grimacing at the pool of bloody rain water trickling out from his clothes. She caught Swift's eye briefly; his expression said everything he didn't. *Be careful. Keep watch.*

She nodded. "I'll see you soon."

Annie had just turned to follow the others when Swift stopped her.

"O'Malley." He had his work voice on.

She turned back. He stood by the kitchen door, his expression was unreadable, but his eyes were alive with worry.

"Give me a second," he said quietly to Peter, then crossed to Annie, his shoes leaving wet prints on the flagstones.

"Be careful," he murmured, voice low enough that only she could hear. "We don't know who's done this yet, and I don't like any of them enough to trust them."

"I'm always careful," she said; she tried to make light, but it wasn't working.

Swift shook his head. "No. I mean it. Someone here knows exactly what happened to Vale. And until we can reach the police, everyone left in this house is a suspect."

Annie followed his gaze through the open doorway, where the others were already drifting back towards the drawing room and the firelight.

Theo, the spurned caterer, who'd looked at Vale's body like a rival, not a victim. Lady Agatha, calm to the point of callous, more worried about scandal than blood, and very quick to stop them from calling for back up. Cassie, her daughter, who had left the dining table just like Theo and returned pale and shaken, the person who had found Vale's dead body. And Noah, the man who had never come back at all.

Annie's stomach twisted. "You think Vale's killer is a danger to us all?"

"I think people who kill are all dangerous," Swift said grimly. "And I think whoever killed Vale might not be finished."

The thunder rolled again, close enough to shake the kitchen windowpanes.

Swift's eyes found hers in the torchlight. "Someone in this house has blood on their hands," he said quietly. “And we can’t leave until we know who.”

Annie swallowed hard, glancing towards the dark corridor that led back to the drawing room. The laughter from earlier had long since died.

She squared her shoulders. “Then I’d better start watching them properly.”

Swift gave a faint, grim smile. “That’s my girl.”

Then he turned back to the body and Annie walked into the waiting dark.

EIGHT

Annie's hair clung to her neck in damp curls, and her shoes squelched faintly on the rug every time she moved. The fire roared in the grate, throwing waves of heat into the air, but even that didn't take the edge off the chill that had settled over the room.

It felt wrong. A body was being carried to the cellar and yet here they were, huddled in cashmere throws, brandy glasses in hand like it was still a dinner party.

Annie moved her feet closer to the fire, glad of its warmth as she slipped out of her shoes and tried to defrost her toes. She was observing them all from her arm chair, trying to work out if any of them looked like a killer. But she knew from experience that it wasn't always easy to spot the black sheep. Theo stood at the window, the curtain pulled back slightly, staring out into the darkness. His shoulders were so tight they were hunched up near his ears. Lady

Agatha sat rigidly in her arm chair, a porcelain cup of tea balanced in her perfectly steady hand. Cassie occupied the sofa opposite, her eyes were raw and swollen. Bea and Colin who were back in the drawing room had thankfully missed all the commotion with their loo break and were deep into the contents of a crystal decanter. Even Alice had been invited to sit and warm up. She'd taken Swift's empty arm chair and was clinging to a glass of brandy like it was a lifeline.

The door creaked open and every head turned. Peter entered first, his previously neat uniform soaked and dishevelled, a dark red stain spreading out across his chest. His face was drawn, the colour of parchment, and he looked about ten years older than he had an hour ago. Swift followed, his expression grim, his wet hair pushed back from his forehead in rough, impatient strokes.

"He's safely stored out of the way." Swift came and stood by the fire, looking out over the rest of the guests. "Well, maybe not safely, given the state he was in. I need to ask that no one goes down there in the meantime, we need to keep him as untouched as possible until the police arrive."

Agatha's voice was crisp. "If they arrive, you mean."

Swift flexed his jaw. "They will arrive, we just need to wait for the roads to clear or the lines to be back up again."

Peter crossed to the fire and Annie could see the

way his hands trembled as he held them out towards the flames.

"Awful," he murmured. "That poor man…" He trailed off, staring into the hearth and the room fell into a thick silence as the guests sipped at their drinks.

"All right," Swift said, breaking the silence. "As we might have a long wait before we can call for help, I think the best thing we can do is start our own investigation. I can't just sit back and feel useless. If I can, I need to work out what happened to Vale and why and to do that I need to ask you all some questions."

Agatha's cup clinked faintly against its saucer. "Joseph, really—"

"I'm not doing this for sport, Lady Agatha," Swift cut in. "You have a dead man in your cellar. And, like it or not, he didn't die from natural causes."

Theo's head jerked around. "Wait—what?"

"Not natural causes?" Cassie's mouth fell open, her voice wavered. "Was it an accident?"

Swift met her eyes evenly. "No, unless he fell numerous times onto his own carving knife, no, I'm almost certain it was not an accident."

Bea let out a small, startled gasp, one hand flying to her throat. "Good heavens."

Colin shifted beside her, his brandy sloshing in the glass. "Bloody hell, Joseph. You might soften the delivery next time."

"You're saying there's a murderer in this house?" Theo's face had gone even paler.

"That's exactly what I'm saying," Swift replied.

"And until we know who, no one leaves, and no one wanders off alone."

The fire cracked sharply, punctuating his words and making Annie flinch.

Cassie stared into her lap, her fingers worrying at the edge of her cardigan. "It might not be someone still in the house, surely? What about all the other guests at dinner?"

A thought smacked at Annie and she looked up sharply. "No," she said. "It can't have been any of the guests who have already gone."

All eyes turned to her. She could feel the heat of the fire on her skin and the weight of their stares all at once.

"How do you know that?" Bea asked, leaning forward, brandy glass forgotten in her hand.

"Because Vale was still alive after the dessert," Annie said. "Remember? He came out with the savoury course, that sharp little cheese thing."

"The rarebit bites," Colin said, snapping his fingers. "Yes! I had three."

"Exactly." Annie nodded. "He was in the room then. That was after the auction and the main meal, when most of the guests had already started leaving because of the storm."

She hesitated, piecing the rest together aloud. "And it was Vale who went to check the generator when the power cut out. Peter said so. Which means he was definitely still alive until the lights went off. And when the lights went off, there was only us left."

The words hung there for a moment, heavy as the storm outside.

"That's right." Swift gave a small nod. "And, I'm no expert, but judging from the body, it happened after the storm cut the power and after the last cars left the grounds. Which narrows the field considerably."

Theo ran a hand through his hair, pacing a few steps. "You make it sound like one of us. Anyone could have stayed after the party, hidden out in this giant, bloody house."

It was plausible, true, but Annie didn't believe it. Swift didn't say anything. He didn't need to.

"Don't be ridiculous." Agatha gave a brittle laugh, the sound cracking in the heavy air. "My daughter, my guests, my staff, none of us are capable of something so barbaric."

"That's what everyone thinks," Annie said quietly. "Until it happens."

No one spoke after that. The wind battered against the windows, and the old clock on the mantel ticked far too loudly. For the first time that night, Annie saw the realisation settle on them. The understanding that this wasn't just gossip or a crime scene on television. They were trapped in a house with a killer. And the storm outside showed no sign of letting up.

Swift straightened from the hearth, the firelight throwing sharp planes of shadow across his face. Annie thought he looked tired but when he spoke, his voice was measured and carried the weight of a man in charge.

"And that," he said, "is exactly why I need to talk to each of you. Just to get a sense of where everyone was when Vale was murdered."

Agatha's eyes narrowed. "You can't possibly think—"

"I don't think anything yet," Swift said evenly. "But I know how investigations work, given it's my job. We establish timelines. We work out who was where, and who wasn't. It's not an accusation, Lady Agatha, it's procedure and I'll also need a list from you of staff who are still here."

Bea glanced nervously at Colin. "Well, I can save you some time. We were right here, drinking this wonderful brandy."

Colin nodded. "Haven't moved since we got back from the powder room, old chap."

Swift allowed himself a flicker of a smile at the old couple. "Good to know. The sooner we have a clear picture, the better. And I am starting to wonder about Noah too. Agatha, I know you said he left as he was feeling unwell, but we can't rule out the fact that he might not have gotten very far. We can talk about the book he was writing about Blackthorn Hall and its history. There was something he wanted to tell me, something he'd found out."

Swift left the unasked question out in the open and turned his attention back to the rest of the guests. Annie could feel the shift in the room as the air tightened around them.

Swift's gaze swept across them all and settled finally on Theo. "Let's begin with you."

All eyes turned to Theo whose pale face pinkened almost immediately. "What? Why me?"

"You're the most obvious suspect, Theo. You were a rival chef, recently replaced by the man now lying dead in the cellar. You had motive and proximity."

Theo's jaw tightened. "So I'm guilty because I'm passionate about my job?"

"I didn't say guilty," Swift said evenly. "I said an obvious suspect."

Theo let out a harsh laugh, rubbing a hand over his face. "Yes, I was annoyed, all right. Vale swoops in from London with his fancy attitude, and suddenly I'm demoted to outside of the kitchen. But being angry doesn't mean I stabbed the guy."

"Well, thank goodness for that," Bea muttered, and Colin shot her a warning look.

Swift tilted his head slightly, his eyes still on Theo. "Then maybe you can explain why you left the dining room in the middle of the meal and came back looking like you'd been caught in the rain?"

Theo's face scrunched. "What?"

"You got up and left during dinner" Swift went on. "Said you needed to make a call. But when you came back, you looked like you'd been out in the rain."

A muscle ticked in Theo's cheek. "I told you; I was trying to get a signal. The Wi-Fi in this mausoleum's useless."

Swift didn't look away. "You didn't think it odd to step outside into a storm for the sake of a phone call?"

Theo's mouth flattened. "I didn't go outside-outside. Just to the back door near the kitchen. I needed some air. I didn't even see Vale. Besides, it wasn't a storm then, it was just a bit of rain and wind. I didn't stab Vale."

"That's good," Agatha murmured.

Theo's head snapped towards her. "Excuse me?"

"Young Joseph here is implying that my hiring a better chef drove you to violence, Mr Morton, that's quite a stretch, but I still would hate to be in any way involved."

"Better?" Theo's laugh was bitter. "He's no better than me, I came up with the menu, he butchered that meat. It was so weird."

"Theo," Cassie said sharply. Her hands were clenched in her lap, her knuckles white. "That's enough."

"All I'm saying is it's not a crime to take a breather."

"Not unless someone dies while you're gone," Colin murmured.

"Someone didn't die while I was gone," Theo spluttered. "Vale was still alive, he must have been because he was still making the dessert. And we all saw him later, didn't we?"

Swift didn't push, just nodded once. "All right. We're done, for now."

Theo sat, muttering something that sounded a lot like witch hunt under his breath. The tension rippled through the room again; Annie caught Swift's eye and he gave her the smallest of smiles. Just enough to let her know she was safe.

Swift shifted his attention. "Miss Blackthorn, Cassie, you also left the table during dinner, didn't you?"

Cassie nodded. "Yes. I went to the ladies' room. That's not a crime."

"Did you see anyone in the corridor?" Annie asked.

"No. It was quite empty." Cassie's gaze flicked briefly to her mother. "And loud. The storm, I mean."

Agatha smiled without looking at her. "My daughter is easily rattled by weather."

Cassie's throat bobbed. "That's not true."

Annie filed away the brittleness between mother and daughter. There had been an atmosphere between the two of them all evening, and Cassie must have been in Lady Agatha's bad books to not be sat at the top table with her. Annie was determined to get to the bottom of what was going on between them.

Swift's eyes narrowed slightly as he carried on questioning Cassie. "And what were you doing outside?"

Cassie's eyes widened. "I told you already, I wasn't outside."

"Not then, perhaps, but you were outside when you found Vale's body, weren't you?"

Colour flared high on Cassie's cheeks. "I—I heard something. A noise at the window. I thought someone was calling for help, so I went to look. It was stupid, I know. I didn't realise—" She broke off, shivering as though the memory itself had teeth.

Agatha's voice sliced through the space between them. "Detective Swift, I think that's quite enough."

Swift didn't turn. "With respect, Lady Agatha, I need to establish where your daughter was and what she saw."

"And with respect to you," Agatha said, rising slightly in her seat, "you are a guest in my home. My daughter has just been through a terrible shock, and she will not be interrogated like a suspect in a police station. If you intend to continue down this line of questioning, I suggest you wait until we've spoken to our lawyers."

The words landed like ice water. Even the fire seemed to dim under them.

Swift's mouth tightened. "Lawyers won't change the facts, Lady Agatha. There's a dead man downstairs and your daughter was the one who found him. That makes her a witness, whether you like it or not."

Agatha didn't blink. "And you, Detective, are not currently on duty. Do not mistake this house for your station."

Annie felt the temperature in the room plummet. For a second, she thought Swift might push harder, he certainly looked like he wanted to. But then he inhaled through his nose and nodded once, backing down with that same grim restraint she'd seen him use when cornered by DCI Robins.

"Fine," he said quietly. "Fine."

The silence that followed was taut enough to snap. Cassie pressed herself back into the sofa, her knuckles white against the brandy glass in her hand. Annie's gaze flicked to Agatha who looked calm and far too composed for a woman whose home held a dead body.

NINE

"I DIDN'T KILL HIM."

Annie had been alone with her thoughts, staring into the roar of the flames as the storm bruised itself against the windows. She was so lost in the rhythm of it that she didn't hear Theo squat down beside her until he spoke.

"Theo." Annie sat back in her chair, watching him. "You look like you have the weight of the world on your shoulders. Is there anything else you want to tell me? Anything to back up your claim?"

Theo dragged a hand down his face and looked around the room. Though the other guests were talking amongst themselves, the room wasn't really large enough to have a private conversation. Annie didn't care.

"If you think I'm going somewhere quieter with you then you can think again," she told him. "You might say you're not a killer but I have been on the receiving end of a lying psychopath too many times to take a stranger's word as gospel anymore. If you've got something to say you can say it right here."

"Fine," Theo huffed. "I argued with Vale this evening, before everything went to hell."

Her pulse kicked up. "Go on."

He moved closer to the fire, the orange light cutting hard across his features. "When I left the table at dinner, I went down to the kitchen. I wanted to tell Vale he was botching my menu and I wanted to know what someone who has no idea how to even sauté vegetables had taken my place at the auction. It wasn't supposed to be like this. This is my domain. Vale coming in, taking credit for my work, it smacks of something… I don't know. It's just not sitting right with me. But do you know what he said? He said Agatha wanted someone with more pedigree." He spat the word like it tasted foul. "Pedigree, really? There was literally no pedigree to that meal other than Pedigree Chum. Anyway, we ended up shouting. I might've grabbed his jacket, but I promise you I left before I did something I couldn't take back."

Annie folded her arms. "And that was the last time you saw him alive?"

He nodded once. "He was still in the kitchen when I walked out. Pissed off, but very much alive."

She studied him for a long moment. He looked exhausted, not like a man capable of stabbing another in such a brutal fashion. Still, she'd seen plenty of ordinary faces hide monstrous things.

Theo broke the silence. "There's something else you should know."

"What?" Annie asked, curious.

He hesitated, dropping his voice until Annie could barely hear him. "Earlier today, I saw Vale outside in the garden with Cassie. They were arguing. Proper arguing. He was saying something about her mother, and she told him to keep his mouth shut. Then she saw me and stormed off. This was before I spoke to him."

Annie looked over at the youngest Blackthorn who was wrapped in a tartan blanket and hugging her arms to herself on the sofa. "Vale and Cassie were arguing?"

Theo nodded but didn't offer any further information. Annie tried to piece it together. Theo and Vale arguing. Cassie sneaking off during dinner. Noah missing and Agatha shutting Swift down every time he mentioned him.

"So," she said slowly. "You're saying you saw Cassie having a row with Vale in the garden. And then you argued with him too? Seems there was a lot of people annoyed with the dead chef."

"Two people," Theo said, his voice cracking. "But I swear to God, Annie, when I left Vale, he was alive."

Annie wanted to believe him. She almost did. But her instincts didn't rest easy after three years on the job.

"Everything all right here?" Swift appeared beside them, a shadow over his face.

Theo straightened. "Just telling Annie here what happened."

Swift's eyes darkened even further. "And what was that?"

Theo's mouth twisted. "Ask Annie, I don't want to talk to you. You think you've already got your man, don't you?"

"I think I've got a man whose job was taken mere days earlier by the person who ended up dead," Swift said evenly. "A man who left the dinner without explanation and came back looking dishevelled. That's not exactly a glowing alibi."

Bea's voice drifted across from the sofa. "Are you going to arrest him, Joe? Because that seems awfully premature."

Swift ignored her. "For everyone's safety, I'd prefer if Theo stayed in one of the bedrooms until morning. Preferably one that can be locked from the outside."

"What?" Theo snapped. "You can't be serious."

Colin sat up straighter. "Theo has a point, young man. You can't just stick him in a room like some murder suspect. This isn't an episode of Sherlock Holmes."

Swift's jaw flexed. "It's temporary. Just until we can reach the authorities."

Bea drained her glass and set it down with a firm clink. "I know you mean well, Joseph, but locking someone up when we're all terrified and trapped already? That's barbaric. We're supposed to be civilised, aren't we?"

Theo shot her a grateful look, then turned back to Swift. "You'll regret this when the truth comes out."

Annie stepped in before Theo could launch into another tirade, or worse.

"Joe," she said quietly. "Can I talk to you? Alone."

Swift looked like he wanted to refuse, but something in her tone must have got through because he gave a tight nod. "Fine. Everyone stay here. Keep an eye on Mr Morton, please."

"We'll chain him to the drink's trolley if he misbehaves." Bea saluted Swift with her glass.

Theo rolled his eyes, muttering something under his breath as Swift ushered Annie towards the door.

It was freezing outside the drawing room and away from the fire. Though Annie had pretty much dried off from earlier, the damp chill had made it all the way to her bones. The storm seemed to be dulled a little, settling into a steady hiss of rain against the old glass. They walked in the pool of light from Annie's phone torch.

"Is everything okay?" Swift asked finally. "You looked like you had something you didn't want to say in front of the rest of them. Is it Theo?"

"Kind of." She kept her voice just above a whisper. "Theo did tell me he argued with Vale tonight. He said he confronted him about taking over the menu.

They shouted, maybe even grabbed each other, but he swears Vale was alive when he left."

Swift exhaled through his nose. "And we're just supposed to take his word for it?"

"There's more." Annie slowed, her light catching on a tall mirror, their reflections ghosted and pale. "Theo said he saw the other chef arguing with Cassie earlier."

Swift frowned. "Vale and Cassie?"

Annie nodded. "He said Cassie told him to keep his mouth shut about something to do with her mother."

For a moment, they walked in silence, the floor creaking beneath their feet.

Swift rubbed the back of his neck. "If Theo's telling the truth, it complicates things. But it doesn't clear him. He had motive, opportunity, and it sounds like he has a hell of a temper."

"And you're planning to lock him up away from everyone else? When we've got no electricity, no phones, no idea who else might be creeping around?" Annie glanced down the shadowed corridor ahead.

Swift's brow furrowed. "But what if he's dangerous?"

"I think we don't know who's dangerous," she said. "There could be all sorts of people hiding in these corridors. Staff we haven't seen, guests who never actually left. If we split everyone up, we're sitting ducks."

Swift stopped walking. The only light between

them came from Annie's phone, the glow turning his eyes an unnatural silver. "So, what do you suggest?"

"We keep everyone together until it's light or the police get through. Locking Theo away might make sense on paper, but if something's moving in this house…"

"Then we're safer where we can see each other," he finished quietly.

"Exactly."

"You're right. I don't like it, but you're right." He rubbed his jaw.

Annie gave him a faint smile. "Not for the first time."

"O'Malley, Annie, I'm sorry for dragging you into this." He leant and gave her a brief kiss, running a hand down her cheek. "Fish and chip Friday from now on. Might even venture as far as Pete's. But no further."

"Trouble is as trouble does, Swift." Annie kissed him back.

They started back down the corridor, the firelight ahead flickering through the half-open door to the drawing room. Then Annie froze. In the tall gilt mirror halfway down the hall, something moved. A shape slid just out of frame, as if it had been standing behind them and ducked away the instant she noticed. Her breath caught. The reflection rippled faintly and for one horrifying second she could have sworn there was a face, pale, expressionless, and far too close to hers.

“Joe,” she whispered. “There’s someone there.”

Swift turned, scanning the corridor. The beam from Annie’s phone torch cut across the empty walls, the closed doors, the glinting mirror. But there was nothing there.

“There’s no one,” he said quietly. “Must have been a shadow.”

Annie didn’t move. The mirror stared back reflecting only them, but she could still feel the static charge in the air.

Swift touched her arm. “Come on.”

She tore her gaze from the glass, forcing herself forward. But as she went, her kitten heel caught on the edge of the rug, sliding right down to her toes. She muttered under her breath and bent to tug her shoe back into place, one hand braced against the wall for balance. Only it wasn’t wall. Something clicked beneath her palm and before she could react, the door swung open. Annie pitched sideways with a startled yelp.

“Annie!” Swift lunged, catching her elbow just as she stumbled into the darkness beyond.

“I’m fine,” she said, though her heart was trying to punch through her ribs. “Bloody hell, I didn’t even see that was a door.”

Swift had lifted his own phone and tapped the torch, swinging the beam around inside. They’d fallen into an office, by the look of it, lined with shelves heaving with books. They stepped in cautiously. The torchlights swept across a heavy desk in the centre, papers scattered like someone had been searching in a hurry. Annie's stomach clenched.

"Swift," she said softly. "Look."

Hung over the back of the chair was a heavy, woollen coat, and beside it a satchel she recognised instantly as the one Noah had been carrying. The contents were tipped across the rug, a notebook, a cracked phone, a wallet curling with damp.

Swift crouched, flipping open the notebook with the edge of his sleeve. "This is soaking wet."

Annie knelt beside him, her skin prickling. "Do you think he's been here recently?"

Swift picked up one of the scattered pages, frowning. "These are notes on the Blackthorn family. Look at the dates and the names." He held the paper closer to the light and Annie could see the writing.

Her throat went dry. "Noah never left, did he?"

"No," Swift said quietly. "I'm starting to think he didn't."

TEN

TOGETHER ANNIE AND SWIFT GATHERED UP NOAH'S things. Annie shoved all of the items strewn across the floor into his satchel, flipping the flap over to keep them safe. She slung it over her shoulder, feeling the weight of it pull hard against her neck. It was heavier than she'd expected, and the smell of damp that clung to it itched the back of her throat.

Swift took the coat and swept the torch once more around the room until he was happy that they had everything.

"I guess we need to work out whether Noah left these in here himself." He frowned. "Or someone else put them here out of the way."

"And no matter the answer to that question, we need to find out where Noah is," Annie said, trying to work out if Noah was a suspect in the death of Vale or at risk himself. "Do you have any idea what he wanted to talk to you about?"

Swift shook his head, his lips pursed. Annie could see the frustration on his face as clearly as if it was written there in ink. She was about to tell him that it wasn't his fault he didn't know where Noah was or what he wanted to offload when her phone buzzed once in her hand, startling her.

Swift turned. "What's that?"

"Signal," she breathed, barely daring to move in case she lost it again. Two bars blinked faintly in the corner of her screen. "Oh my God, I've got a connection to the outside world."

"Yes, Annie, get a message out," Swift said. "Get backup."

She opened WhatsApp and typed into their MCU group chat as fast as her numb fingers would allow.

> Emergency. Blackthorn Hall. Storm, power out, one dead, we're trapped. Lines down, roads blocked. Send help ASAP. Photo of deceased attached.

She added one of the pictures of Vale and hit send. The message blinked, hung, then went grey, a clock symbol in the corner.

"Come on," she muttered. "Come on, come on—"

Swift angled his own phone, but his screen stayed blank. "Nothing here."

"It's sending," Annie said, staring at her screen as if sheer willpower could push it through. "I wish it would go because I'm getting cramp in my hand from staying so still."

Swift stepped in beside her, one hand hovering just over her shoulder as if touching her might jinx the connection. The little clock icon on her message flashed then vanished and a double grey tick appeared.

"Yes," Annie hissed. "It's sent."

"Let's hope Tink and Page aren't asleep."

Annie looked at the time, surprised to see it was almost 2am. "Shit," she said. "What if they are?"

"Then they'll see it in the morning," Swift said. "And we've done what we can. Let's get these bits back to the fire, it's bloody freezing and I've got some questions about Noah that I'd like to ask Lady Agatha."

They started back down the corridor, their torches cutting through the dark until the firelight from the drawing room grew brighter. Inside the drawing room, the atmosphere had shifted. Annie felt it almost immediately. There was a tautness to the air that was pulled so tightly it made it hard to get further than the door.

"Everything okay in here?" she asked, looking around at the guests.

Theo was perched on the arm of a chair, still simmering quietly. Bea and Colin both looked as drained as their empty glasses, their age showing in the early morning hour. Cassie sat curled beneath a throw, her eyes glassy and fixed on the flames. And Lady Agatha stood by the mantel, staring at her daughter with a frown. It was amazing to Annie that Peter and Alice were still in the room, they hardly took up any of the space at all, despite there being two of them. So used to having to blend into the background, Annie wished they'd make themselves comfortable and join in with the guests. It wasn't normal circumstances, after all.

Colin was the first to speak, his voice sounded gravelly. "We were hoping to get a bit of sleep, if that's allowed. Thought we might make up a few beds in here as we didn't fancy wandering off anywhere."

"Not after everything that's happened," Bea added. "Besides, it's warmer here. We'll make do with the sofas."

"That's a good idea." Annie nodded. "The rest of the house is absolutely freezing."

Agatha's head snapped round, her frown deepening. "I'm aware of the temperature, Miss O'Malley. My staff is small, and we can hardly keep every fire lit in a place this size. Not since the pandemic. Or the ridiculous rise in energy bills. Peter and Alice, fetch some blankets."

They scuttled from the room like mice.

"Of course, Lady Agatha," Annie said quickly, forcing a small smile. "I didn't mean anything by it. Just that it's best for everyone to stay in here."

"Good," Agatha said, turning back towards the fire with the air of someone reclaiming lost ground.

Annie exchanged a brief glance with Swift, who had been studying Lady Agatha. Annie wasn't sure what surprised her more, the speed of Agatha's defensiveness, or the guilt threaded through it. It was as if every throwaway comment was a personal accusation towards her and Blackthorn Hall.

Swift ignored the barb as he set Noah's coat on the nearest chair. Annie placed the satchel on the seat and dragged the chair nearer the fire to dry off the contents.

"We found this in an office off the main corridor. It's Noah's coat and satchel. Looks like he never left the house after all."

Cassie sat upright, glaring at her mother. "What? But you said he had left."

If Annie didn't know better, she'd say that Cassie looked frightened. But why?

"Everything was tipped out of his bag," Annie told Agatha. "Like someone was searching in it."

Bea leaned forward, curiosity overcoming her tiredness. "Searching for what?"

"We don't know," Annie said. "But there were notes on the family, by the looks of it."

Agatha's expression flickered, just for a second. "Of course there were notes, he's writing a book about us. That's the room he is working in."

Bea leant forward and tried to take hold of the satchel, but Annie moved it just out of her reach. There was no reason for her to need to take a closer look and no reason for Annie to let her. A man had died, and this could be evidence as far as she knew. Best to let as few people as possible touch the satchel until they found Noah and could cross him off their list.

"Why's he wondering around when he could be here in the warmth with us? Bit weird, if you ask me," Theo muttered.

"Then it's good no one did ask you," Agatha snapped and the tension in the room sharpened again.

Annie crouched beside the fire, letting the heat hit her face while she thumbed at her phone. The signal had gone again and she had no way of telling who, if anyone, had read their call for help. She had no idea who she could trust, besides Swift. Every single one of them was acting weird and Annie would rather take her chances and sleep outside in the storm than in here with these five strangers.

Sadly for her, Swift had other ideas.

They began to make up beds, or as close to beds as they could manage. Peter and Alice returned with extra blankets and some pillows. They didn't stop long enough to talk though, and Annie noted how pale and drawn Alice looked as she and Peter slipped out the room.

Bea and Colin were on one of the sofas, Cassie and Agatha on the other, and Theo took the wingback next to the fire. Annie sank onto the rug, half-wrapped in a throw that smelled faintly of old perfume as Swift checked the locks on the windows. Her legs ached. Her brain was thick with exhaustion and adrenaline and maybe still the effects of too many glasses of champagne. All she wanted to do was close her eyes and sleep, and hopefully wake up in her own bed with Sunday the cat swatting her face for breakfast like normal.

But as the wind screamed down the chimneys like a living thing, rattling the fire screen so hard that sparks spat out of the grate, Annie knew that sleep wasn't going to be easy. She pulled the throw tighter around her shoulders and stared into the flames. Each new gust of wind made the fire gutter and flare.

Swift finished his circuit of the windows and returned to her side. He lowered himself onto the rug beside her, stretching his long legs towards the hearth. The warmth touched his face, but it didn't soften his expression.

"Windows are secure," he murmured.

"What's going on here, Joe? I don't like it, it feels weird," she said, her voice low enough that it wouldn't carry.

"I know, I feel the same," he said, and then caught himself, offering a faint smile. "Try to sleep, Annie, I'm going to stay awake and make sure no one gets in… or out."

She huffed a small laugh—though it caught in her throat—and snuggled into his chest. The contact was grounding, it felt solid and human, warm in a room that felt increasingly like a cell. Annie wanted to stay awake and keep watch too, but exhaustion was pulling her under in slow, irresistible waves. Her body felt heavier by the minute, and her mind began to fog around the edges. The storm became a rhythm, a steady, violent lullaby. She let her eyes close for what she told herself would be only a second. But time slipped away.

The next sound she heard wasn't the storm, it was a floorboard creaking beneath a cautious foot, and Annie's eyes snapped open.

The fire had burned lower, more ember than flame now. The room was bathed in a deep, red glow that made everything seem slightly unreal. Across the hearth, Bea and Colin lay entwined on the sofa under a blanket, their breathing slow and deep. Lady Agatha sat upright, head tilted slightly forward, as though she'd fallen asleep mid-guard duty. Swift was snoring behind her, also unable to stave off the exhaustion. Annie didn't move. She let her lashes lift a fraction and pretended to still be asleep.

Her heart picked up. Someone was moving in the shadows. Her gaze shifting slightly, Annie caught sight of a shape and squinted to see it better. It was Theo. He was standing half in shadow, one hand resting on the back of the wingback chair he'd been sitting in earlier. His head turned towards the hallway, listening. Annie couldn't see his face properly, but she saw the tension in his shoulders.

Then, slowly, he moved.

Barely a sound, but the air seemed to change with him. The latch of the door clicked, soft as a sigh, and the door opened just wide enough to let a sliver of hallway darkness in.

But before Annie could wake Swift, another shadow stirred.

From the sofa opposite, Cassie rose, ghostlike, her throw sliding to the floor in a silent puddle of fabric. Her hair, half-fallen from its pins, gleamed dark in the dying firelight. Cassie moved then, quickly and quietly, and followed Theo to the door and they both vanished out into the corridor.

Annie made a split-second decision to leave Swift sleeping and instead, slid the throw from her lap inch by inch, trying not to make a sound. She crouched low, her muscles stiff from the cold, and crept towards the door. The rug muffled her steps, but her heart was pounding so loudly it felt like it might wake the entire house.

At the doorway, she paused, peering out.

The corridor beyond was drenched in darkness except for the occasional flash of lightning through the tall window at the end. It strobed the hallway, white, black, white again, each burst revealing empty space.

She turned back for one last glance at the room behind her. Everyone was still asleep, and then she stepped out into the hall, pulling the door quietly shut behind her.

ELEVEN

Lightning split across the windows again, bleaching the corridor bone-white. For a heartbeat she thought she saw Cassie's dress flash near the far end, but by the time thunder rolled through, the space was empty.

Annie started forward slowly, her bare feet whispering across the rugs. Kicking herself, Annie realised in her haste she'd left her phone in the drawing room, beside Swift. *Idiot.* The next flash of lightning gave her just enough to glimpse the turn in the corridor, past the office where they'd found Noah's belongings.

She hesitated there, listening. But there was nothing. Only the faint, irregular thump of the storm and the noises that old buildings make in the night. She pressed herself against the wall, feeling the cold seeping through the plaster.

A floorboard creaked somewhere ahead and Annie's breath snagged.

"Cassie?" she whispered, but her voice came out as a dry rasp. "Theo?"

No answer. The silence that followed was so complete it felt alive. Then something filled it. And, this time, it sounded like more footsteps. Her stomach turned to ice.

She pressed her back to the wall, straining her eyes against the dark. A shape flickered at the far end of the hall, or maybe it was just her eyes playing tricks on her in the dark again, she couldn't tell. But every instinct she had was screaming at her to run.

A bolt of lightning ripped through the sky outside, flooding the corridor in blinding white light. For a single, frozen heartbeat, Annie saw the outline of a person, but it was wrong in every way that mattered. Too tall, too thin. Its edges seemed to shimmer, blurred by the rain-streaked window behind it. The face was leached of colour; a ghastly oval suspended in the flash. Its eyes gleamed like wet stone. And then the light vanished, plunging the hall back into suffocating black.

Annie's breath tore from her chest in a broken gasp. She didn't wait to find out if it was real. Too scared by what she had seen, she span and ran back to the safety of the drawing room.

Her bare feet slipped on the rug as she sprinted away, every nerve screaming that the thing she'd seen was right behind her. She could feel its breath on her neck. Hot and pungent. The corridor stretched endlessly ahead, flashes of lightning chasing her shadow along the walls.

She reached the door, fumbled for the handle, and shoved it open so hard it slammed against the wall. The thunder rolled overhead as she stumbled inside and slammed it shut again, chest heaving, heart hammering. Yet the others slept on, undisturbed.

Annie pressed her back to the door, trying to steady her breath.

Whatever she'd heard, or seen, out there, she wasn't going to wake the house over it. Now she was in the safety of the others, Annie felt stupid to think that there were monsters creeping around the corridors. She crept back across the room and tucked herself down beside Swift again, letting the heat of the fire and his body chase some of the chill from her skin.

She stared into the dying embers, forcing her thoughts to slow. What the hell were Cassie and Theo doing sneaking off together? And why had Cassie looked so afraid when they'd mentioned Noah earlier? But her eyelids grew heavy again and eventually, exhaustion won.

The next thing Annie knew, sunlight was streaming across her face.

She flinched, instinctively shielding her eyes. For a disorienting second, she had no idea where she was. But the taste of old champagne on her tongue soon pulled it all back. The worst of the storm had passed and outside, birds were chattering in the rain.

Swift stirred beside her. "Morning?" he croaked, his voice rough.

"Apparently." She stretched her stiff arms, feeling every bone in her neck complain. "How did you sleep?"

"Like a corpse. Which, given the circumstances, I'm not sure is a good sign." He yawned and rubbed his face. "You alright?"

Annie hesitated, looking around to make sure everyone else was still asleep. Cassie and Theo were back in their respective beds as though they hadn't snuck out together.

"Not really." She lowered her voice. "I saw something last night."

That woke him properly. He sat up, watching her intently. "What kind of something?"

"Theo and Cassie." She took a breath. "They left the room after everyone else was asleep. I followed them but lost them—"

"You followed them? Alone? Annie!"

"I'm fine," Annie whispered, a cold chill making her shudder as she remembered the weird creature in the corridor. "But as I say, I lost them, I couldn't see a thing without my phone."

Swift frowned. "Did they leave at the same time or together?"

"Together, definitely. It looked like Theo waited for Cassie at the door."

Swift rubbed the bridge of his nose. "That's interesting, I didn't think they knew each other well enough to be sneaking around."

"Exactly." Annie leaned forward and lowered her voice even further as Agatha let out a snore. "What do you think is going on? Do you think they've got something to do with Vale's death?"

"I don't know." He glanced towards the sofa where Cassie still slept under her blanket, one hand tucked beneath her chin like a child. "But do you remember her mentioning a man she was getting married to, back at the dinner table?"

Annie nodded. "You think it's Theo?"

Swift rubbed his jaw, eyes narrowing as he stared towards the dying embers in the hearth. He got up and placed another log on them, blowing the base to ignite what was still burning. Soon the flames started to lick around the new logs and Annie could feel the warmth on her toes. Swift sat on the free armchair and rubbed his hands together over the flames.

"It's possible," he whispered, eyes darting around the room. "But before we start making assumptions, we need to look at what we've actually got." He nodded at the chair where Noah's satchel sat drying. "Maybe whatever Noah was working on rattled someone enough to make him disappear. If we look properly at what's in that notebook, maybe we'll see what he uncovered."

"Good idea." Annie started to get up to go and lift the notebook out the bag when she saw Swift hesitate. "What?"

His eyes had drifted to the window, where the light leaking through the gap in the curtains was still pale and flat.

"I've got a bad feeling," he said finally. "About Vale's body."

"Bad feeling?" she repeated. "What do you mean?"

"Honestly, I'm not entirely sure." He prodded at the fire with the iron poker, sending sparks flying up into the chimney. "Only that I think I made a mistake leaving a victim's body without a guard. If the killer is still amongst us, and I am pretty sure they are, then they'll know they need to remove all traces of evidence, and I basically gave them free rein to do so last night."

"Swift, you can't blame yourself, you're doing the best you can with the tools you've been given. You couldn't exactly bring Vale's body up here to watch over, imagine what the heat of the fire would have done to it." Annie didn't really want to picture it.

"I could have stayed down in the cellar with him," Swift replied.

"And got pneumonia? You'd have been no good to anyone if so. Or as dead as Vale. No, stop it, Joe, there's no need to give yourself a hard time."

"I don't know," Swift admitted, standing. "I need to go and check."

Annie pushed herself upright quickly with a groan, her joints stiff from the night on the floor. "Well, don't think you're going down there alone."

"Didn't think you'd let me." He gave her a look she knew well.

"No bloody way." She brushed off her dress and reached for her shoes. "Let's make it quick, though, before anyone else wakes up."

They slipped from the drawing room into the corridor, the silence of morning pressing close around them. The storm had blown itself out, but the aftermath lingered in the puddles glinting on the flagstones outside and the faint smell of ozone in the air. They moved carefully through the hallways that seemed familiar now. Annie had been here less than twenty-four hours, and already it felt like a lifetime.

They reached the door to the cellar stairs and Swift paused, one hand on the wood. "You ready?"

"Define ready."

He smiled faintly, pushed open the door, and started down the stairs. The air grew colder as they descended, and as they reached the bottom and stepped into the small wine cellar, Swift flicked on his phone torch and Vale's covered body came into view. Blood had started to seep through the towels and made a grim sight. Annie shivered so violently she slipped down the last step. Swift grabbed her elbow and stopped her falling right on top of the dead chef.

"Thanks," she whispered. Her heart was hammering so loudly in her chest she barely heard the other noise over the sound of it. "Swift, what's that?"

Swift paused. "What?"

"Footsteps."

He turned, listening, one hand still on Annie's arm, and Annie heard it louder now. Soft, uneven steps descending behind them. A moment later, a familiar voice echoed down the stairwell.

"Wait, Swift! Annie!"

Swift exhaled. "Theo."

The chef appeared in the doorway, looking rumpled and uneasy, one hand clutching the banister.

"Sorry," he said quickly. "I didn't mean to startle you."

"You did anyway," Annie muttered. "What are you doing down here?"

Theo ran a hand through his hair. "I needed to talk to you. I've been thinking about yesterday. About the argument I had with Vale."

He looked over Swift's shoulder and his face paled at the sight of Vale's body.

"Go on." Swift straightened, almost blocking Theo's view.

Theo swallowed. "The thing is… the more I think about it, the more I'm not sure that man was Vale at all."

Annie blinked. "What are you talking about? You said you knew him."

"I'd heard of Soren Vale the chef, yes," Theo said. "But I'd never met the guy before yesterday. And something was off with him. Vale was known to be a bit of a maverick breaking into the culinary world, but he was also a perfectionist. The guy last night was clumsy; his chopping skills lacked finesse and don't even get me started on how he prepped the meat. Like, I'm not even sure he aged it at all. And some of the terms he used when we argued made him sound like an extra on Masterchef, we don't talk like that all the time."

Annie crossed her arms as her stomach let out a painful growl. The memory of the plates of meat she'd drooled over last night pretty vivid in her mind. She would kill for a bacon sandwich, well, maybe not kill for it, but she was really hungry.

"So now you're saying he wasn't who he said he was?" she asked, keen to get out the cellar.

Theo nodded. "Exactly. I don't know who that man was, but I don't think he was Soren Vale."

Annie's mouth went dry. "So whoever that is under those towels could've taken Vale's name and his job? Why?"

"Exactly," Theo said. "Someone wanted to be here under that identity. Maybe they wanted to get close to the family. It's hard getting an invite to one of their parties, even when a charity auction is involved."

"So maybe that was their only way in?" Swift's hand tightened on his phone. "And now that someone's dead." He swung the light around to Theo's face. "What were you doing last night?"

"What?" The chef held up a hand to shield his eyes from the glare of the torch.

"You and Cassie," Swift went on. "You left the room together. Care to explain why?"

Colour surged into Theo's cheeks. "We weren't *together*," he said too quickly. "We just… we both needed the loo, all right? It was a coincidence."

Annie arched a brow. "You just both so happened to be awake at four in the morning?"

Theo's gaze flicked between them, defensive now. "You're making it sound like something it isn't. I didn't kill Vale, and I didn't sneak around with Cassie. I just—" He broke off, shaking his head. "I can't do this down here. Not next to him."

He gestured towards the covered body and the darkened towels, the glistening floor underneath him.

"Then go," Swift said quietly. "Head back upstairs. Annie will go with you."

Theo hesitated, then nodded, relief flickering over his face. He moved for the stairs, muttering something under his breath about this being a nightmare.

Annie turned on Swift. "You're staying?"

"I'm just going to give the body a once over." Swift's tone was grim. "I want to be sure no one's tampered with him."

"Joe—"

He cut her off gently. "Go on. Get Noah's notebook. I think it's all connected—Vale, Noah, Theo, Cassie, whatever's happening here. Keep it safe."

"I don't like leaving you down here alone." Annie hesitated.

Swift glanced up at her, his expression softening just a fraction. "I'm not alone. I've got Vale. Annie, go, quickly before Theo gets away."

She took a step backward, then another, until she was climbing the stairs. Halfway up, she glanced back one last time. Swift was kneeling beside the corpse, his torch beam steady over the blood-dark towel, and a sudden, hollow fear struck her that when she came back, Swift might not be there waiting for her.

TWELVE

ANNIE HAD NO CHOICE BUT TO SHRUG OFF THE feeling and skipped up the stairs after Theo.

"Wait up," she called. "It's dark down here."

Theo didn't wait. Annie muttered expletives under her breath and ran the last few steps to the door and the corridor that was now flooded with morning light.

"You're not doing yourself any favours acting like a total knob, you know," she shouted to him, huffing at the exertion.

As Annie caught up to him, more angry words formed on her tongue, but they stalled when she got a proper look at him. Theo wasn't running away, he looked wrecked. His skin had gone an odd, greyish hue, and his eyes were glassy, staring somewhere beyond her. His hands were trembling slightly, though he tried to hide it by shoving them deep into his pockets.

She couldn't help but soften. "Hey," she said, a little quieter. "I get it. It's a lot to take in."

He gave a shaky laugh that didn't reach his eyes. "You think? I cook for a living, Annie. I slice meat from cows and pigs, not… not that." He swallowed hard, rubbing the back of his neck. "That was a human being. I don't know how you do it. How do you get used to seeing people like that?"

Annie felt the familiar sting of memory of her first crime scene, the copper tang in the air, the way it stayed with you no matter how many showers you took afterwards.

"You don't," she said quietly.

Theo looked at her properly then, and for a second the arrogance she'd come to expect from him dropped away, leaving something raw. Annie nodded at him, no words needed. He exhaled slowly, his shoulders sagging as if the fight had gone out of him.

"I just need some normality," he said, voice rough. "And I'm desperate for some coffee. Maybe then my brain will stop short circuiting."

"Yeah," Annie said, managing a small smile. "Coffee sounds good. The strongest we can make."

He gave a short, humourless laugh. "I don't even know where the bloody machine is in this place."

"Then let's go ask Lady Agatha," Annie said, nodding in the direction of the hallway. "If anyone knows where caffeine lives in this mausoleum, it's her."

"If she doesn't bite our heads off for asking." Theo pushed a hand through his hair.

Annie started down the corridor beside him. "If she does, I'll distract her. You make a run for the espresso."

He huffed another quiet laugh, and for the first time since they'd found Vale's body, the tension between them eased, even if it was just slightly. Annie shoved her hands under her armpits to warm them up, glancing sideways at Theo.

"So," she said, "you and Cassie. You're sure it was just a bathroom break?"

Theo let out a groan. "You're not going to let that go, are you?"

"Not a chance," Annie said lightly. "You both left at the same time. It was in the middle of the night. You must admit, it looks a bit dodgy from where I'm standing."

"It wasn't like that," he said quickly. "Honestly. I couldn't sleep, I got up to use the loo, and she must've had the same idea. That's it. She asked me to wait for her, must have seen me get up."

Annie raised a brow. "That's one hell of a coincidence."

Theo gave her a look somewhere between tired and pleading. "I swear, Annie. I barely know her. What else would we be doing?"

She studied him for a moment longer, then nodded slowly. "All right. But maybe stop being such a tit around others, yeah? Then we might have a tendency to not think the worst about you."

Theo grimaced but he didn't disagree.

Annie pushed open the door to the drawing room and ushered Theo back inside. Bea and Colin were still curled together, a snoring heap under their covers. Cassie had moved to the fireplace and was leaning in so far, Annie was surprised her blanket hadn't caught alight. She turned to ask Agatha about the coffee but the lady of the house's chair was empty. Annie's brow furrowed and she stepped fully into the room, trying to make her voice sound casual, even though something about that empty chair set her teeth on edge.

"Morning," she said, crossing to where Cassie hovered by the fire. The girl's face was pale, her eyes rimmed pink, whether from tears or lack of sleep, Annie couldn't tell. "Warming up?"

Cassie startled slightly, as if she hadn't heard Annie come in. "Oh. Yeah. Couldn't get warm all night."

Annie nodded, crouching beside the chair where Noah's satchel still rested. She lifted it gently onto her knees and started rummaging inside, careful not to look like she was prying even though, technically, she was. "You haven't seen your mum, have you?" she asked lightly.

Cassie frowned, straightening a little. "My mum? I think she said something about finding Peter and

Alice for breakfast." She glanced towards the empty chair, brow furrowed.

"Oh, that's good then," Annie went on. "Theo and I were just wondering about coffee."

Cassie nodded but didn't add anything else to the conversation.

"Go and warm up," she said to Theo and then slid the notebook out of Noah's satchel and kept it tucked against her ribs like contraband.

She tried not to make too big a deal of it, she rose with it grabbing a blanket and clamping it across her shoulders to hide the notebook, and crossed to the little table beside the tall windows. The glass was milky with condensation and a draught crept from the sash, needling the skin at the back of her neck. Pulling the blanket tighter, she opened the book and started to try and make sense of it.

Swift slipped back in to the room a minute or two later, closing the door on a curl of chill from the corridor. His eyes landed on the notebook in Annie's hands and he came straight to her.

"How did you get on?" she whispered.

"Okay," he said, dropping into the chair opposite. "From what I can tell, the body hasn't been tampered with. But it's hard to be sure. We just need to keep an eye on everyone, I guess, to make sure no one else leaves this room. Wait, where's Agatha?"

"Gone to sort out some breakfast, according to Cassie," she said, attempting a smile. "Weird though, seeing as last night the staff seemed to know what she was going to ask for before she'd even opened her mouth. You'd think they'd be on it with some toast at least."

"Or coffee."

"Yeah, that's what Theo and I thought too."

Swift looked over at Theo who was standing warming himself beside the fire. Annie looked too, noticing the way Cassie was staring at the chef with eyes like the daggers in the knife roll.

"What is going on between those two?" Swift whispered. "Did Theo say anything?"

"Just that it was a toilet stop," Annie shook her head. "He was pretty convincing."

Swift hummed in a way that told Annie he believed that as much as he believed in Father Christmas. Who would hopefully be delivering some exciting presents in a few weeks, real or not, if they both got out of here alive.

Swift reached across, rubbing her forearms briskly through the blanket. "What've you got?"

Annie opened the notebook carefully. The pages were swollen; edges frilled with damp. Noah's handwriting slanted to the right but ink was blotted in places where rain had soaked into the paper.

She flipped past family trees and dates and notes that all looked fairly innocuous, until she landed on a section titled

RECENT HISTORY

"Look at this," she murmured, angling the notebook so Swift could see. "Looks like Noah had only just arrived at Lady Agatha's time at the hall."

Swift leaned closer and as he studied the page, Annie studied the whorl of hair at the crown of his head. It was so familiar to her now, the sight made her close her eyes momentarily and pretend she was anywhere other than a freezing cold, murder hall.

"What the…?"

That drew Annie back to the here and now. Swift was tapping a page with the tip of his forefinger. The page was a dense patchwork of arrows, boxed notes, and scrawled writing. He traced a line with his finger.

"This bit, here, it's the timeline of Agatha and her husband." Names, dates, and question marks ran down the page in a jagged column.

1997 – Lord G. Blackthorn inherits Hall

2003 – marries Agatha H

2010 – Loan?

2013 – Trust fund collapsed? (WHY?)

2015 – Staff reduction x 12

2017 – Rumours of defaulting on loan

2019 – Eviction order?? publicly framed as voluntary downsizing? Doesn't add up.

2020 – Hall 'gifted back' after settlement to Lord B

2025 – Lord Blackthorn dies, ownership reverts back to F? Look into marriage clause

---

"Bloody hell." Swift exhaled slowly, his jaw tightening. "This paints a pretty grim picture."

"It explains why she's been so tense whenever you bring up Noah, right?" Annie said quietly. "She's hiding something. And Noah has uncovered that maybe Agatha isn't all she's cracked up to be?"

"I'm worried about Noah." Swift tapped the page again and started to flick forward through the notebook, but there wasn't much else left to read.

Whatever Noah had uncovered, it had rattled Agatha. And Swift was right to be worried about his old friend. Noah had been digging hard, and Agatha's every reaction last night suddenly made awful, perfect sense.

Annie pulled the blanket closer around her shoulders, her teeth beginning to chatter again. Swift noticed and angled his chair closer, their knees brushing. It should've comforted her, but nothing about this place felt comforting anymore.

"We need to talk to Cassie," Swift murmured. "Whatever Noah found, she might've known about it too and —"

He didn't get to finish. A violent crash exploded above their heads. The sounds of glass smashing and falling to the floor. Something heavy hit the floorboards above, hard enough to rattle the chandelier. Swift was on his feet in an instant, eyes flicking straight up to the high ceiling where dust drifted down in a thin, trembling curtain.

"What the hell was that?" Colin croaked from the sofa, scrambling upright as Bea blinked blearily beside him.

But it was Cassie who caught Annie's attention. Her face drained of colour so fast Annie thought she might faint.

"That—" Cassie choked, already stumbling towards the door. "That's my mum's room!"

She hauled the door open and ran out into the corridor.

Swift and Annie shot after her, Noah's notebook forgotten on the table. Annie's pulse hammered against her ribs as she followed Cassie into the corridor, the cold air outside the drawing room slapping her alert in an instant.

"Cassie! Wait!" Swift shouted, taking the stairs two at a time after the young girl.

Cassie was already halfway up the sweeping staircase. Annie grabbed the banister and hauled herself up the last few steps, Swift only a few strides ahead of her now. Cassie reached the landing first, turning sharply back on herself and running towards a closed door.

"Cassie, stop," Swift shouted again.

She didn't listen. She shoved open the door so hard it cracked against the wall behind it. Annie skidded to a halt, almost crashing into the back of Swift. They all looked into the bedroom with wide eyes.

The room looked like a bomb had gone off. A wardrobe lay on its side, one massive oak door torn off its hinges, splintered across the floor. A gigantic mirror had shattered, strewing glittering shards across the rug. But it wasn't the mess that made Annie's skin crawl. It was the emptiness of the room.

Something was very, very wrong and Lady Agatha was nowhere to be seen.

THIRTEEN

Cassie clung to the doorframe as though it were the only thing keeping her upright, then suddenly she was moving.

"Mum?" Her voice cracked as she lunged into the destroyed room, pushing past Swift before he could stop her. "Mum! Mum, are you under there?"

"Cassie, hang on," Swift tried, but she was already dropping to her knees beside the fallen wardrobe, yanking at splintered wood and handfuls of scattered clothes. "There's broken glass everywhere."

"Cassie, please be careful." Annie rushed to the woman's side, trying and failing to stop her from pulling at the broken wood.

But Cassie wasn't listening. She shoved aside a drawer that had burst open, flung aside the broken mirror frame, scrabbled blindly through the heap of clothes and smashed glass.

"Mum!" she cried again, the word shattering in her throat. "Please— please—"

"Cassie." Swift crouched beside her, trying to steady her before she cut herself on the glass. "Stop, you're going to hurt yourself."

"I don't care!" Cassie snapped, shaking him off. "She could be under here!"

"There's no one under here," Annie said softly, scanning the debris. "Cassie, look at me. Your mum is not in the room."

Cassie froze, breathing hard, her fingers still buried in the mess. For a moment she looked like she might be sick. Then footsteps pounded along the landing towards them.

"What's going on?" Bea gasped as she reached the door, Colin right behind her, clutching at his chest.

Great, Annie thought. *The last thing we need is Colin having a coronary when there's enough to contend with already.*

Where were the people in charge? Annie didn't want it to be left to her and Swift because their jobs gave them a sort of authority. So, she actively huffed out a sigh of relief at the sight of Peter's face at the door. Alice was two steps behind him, eyes wide as saucers.

"What's happened?" Peter panted, taking in the broken furniture. "Is Lady Agatha all right?"

Cassie turned on him, running to the door. "Have you seen her? Did she come downstairs? Did she go back to the kitchen?"

Peter flinched at the ferocity in her voice. "N–no. I've been in the laundry room, trying to sort out the leak in the roof tiles. We haven't seen Lady Agatha this morning, I assumed she was still with all of you."

Alice clasped her hands under her chin. "We didn't hear anything. Oh God, has she had a fall?"

"A fall?" Annie repeated, raising an eyebrow at the destroyed wardrobe. "That would have to be some hell of a fall."

Peter and Alice exchanged a look, it was fleeting, but caught easily by Annie's trained eye. Guilt? Fear? Something else? Everyone here seemed to be hiding something and Annie's mind was whirring at a million miles an hour trying to work out how all this mess (literally and figuratively) was connected.

"Let's not crowd the scene," Swift said, throwing his shoulders back. "Everyone back downstairs. We need to regroup."

Swift obviously had no qualms about taking charge.

Cassie's breath hitched. "I'm not leaving! My mum is—"

"Cassie." Swift stepped up to his old friend, his voice gentling. "We'll find her. But right now, I need you safe, all right. Just for a minute while we figure out what we're looking at."

Cassie's chin trembled, but she nodded once.

Swift turned to the others. "Everyone except Cassie needs to head back downstairs. Bea, Colin, take it slow on the steps."

The older couple looked ashen in the dim light seeping through the window, their hands gripping each other as though their joints might give out beneath them. Annie's chest tightened. A night shivering on a sofa, almost no sleep, and now this? They looked brittle enough to blow away like dust.

Swift glanced at Peter. "Can you sort out someone to make breakfast? Something hot. And a large pot of coffee too, please."

Peter's mouth opened, then closed. Alice shifted beside him, wringing her hands.

"Sir… it's just us," she said finally, her voice small.

"What do you mean, just you?"

Peter swallowed hard. "Staff. It's only me and Alice now. Lady Agatha let everyone else go at the beginning of the year. Groundskeepers, kitchen team, the house manager, everyone else has gone."

"We've been doing the work of ten people," Alice whispered, cheeks reddening with the confession. "It's not easy keeping the hall running. Especially with the size of it and everything else."

Weird didn't even begin to cover it. Annie shot Swift a look, mirrored by his subtle tightening jaw. This was another puzzle piece slipping into place. Another hint that the grim picture Noah had written about wasn't just theoretical scribbles in a notebook.

"Right," Swift said, recovering quickly. "In that case, can you take Bea and Colin back downstairs. Get some porridge into them, please. Theo, you too."

"Of course." Peter nodded, moving at once to usher the older couple gently down the stairs.

Bea clutched at his arm gratefully, Colin taking Alice's. Ever the stoic, the old man didn't complain, but his pallor told Annie the cold night had taken more out of him than his pride could hide. Theo followed behind them all, murmuring something Annie couldn't quite grasp, but it was quite obvious he wasn't heeding her words about not being a dick.

When the last footsteps faded down the stairs, the room fell quiet. Cassie remained rooted to the threshold, her fingers dug into the carved wood so tightly her knuckles had gone white.

"Cassie," Swift said gently, "can we talk to you for a minute?"

Cassie frowned. "Is this about my mum? Have you found something? Why aren't we looking for her? What do you know?"

She looked at them with wide, panicked eyes.

"Nothing Cassie, nothing at all," Annie said, keeping her voice even. "We will find your mum. We just need to ask you something first."

Cassie's shoulders bunched, defensive before they'd even begun.

Swift softened his posture, lowering his tone. "Cass, do you know anything about Blackthorn Hall's finances? About your mum facing debts? Or possibly losing the estate?"

"What?" she breathed. "No. No, that's... that's ridiculous. What do you mean?"

Annie watched her closely. The shock seemed real, but so did the flicker underneath it. That tiny tremor of recognition Cassie hadn't managed to hide fast enough.

"We're not accusing anyone," Annie said carefully. "We're trying to understand what is going on here. We have a dead chef, your mum has vanished, and we think Noah disappeared last night too. We're just trying to work out how all this fits together."

"Noah." Cassie's face twisted as though the name itself hurt. "What's Noah got to do with this?"

"We found his notebook," Swift told her. "He seemed to think that Blackthorn Hall, and your mum, are in dire straits financially."

"And you believe that? He is sticking his nose in places it doesn't belong. My family is none of his business. Or yours."

"Cassie," Swift tried again.

"No!" She stepped back, the tremble now shaking her whole frame. "You saw how much money mum raised for charity last night. Why would she do that if she couldn't afford it herself? Why would she still be putting herself out there and inviting people into her home if it's not ours anymore? You were more than happy to accept the invitation, drink our alcohol, eat our food, so don't you dare say that we're broke. Do you know what that could do to our reputation. Noah should have stopped when—"

Cassie snapped her lips shut, not wanting to finish her sentence and Annie's senses pricked.

"Should have stopped when what, Cassie?" Annie reached for her arm.

Cassie wrenched away as though burned. "Stop interfering. Just stop. You're making everything worse."

Then she turned and fled, bolting down the landing and vanishing around the corner before either of them could stop her. For a heartbeat the silence swallowed everything. Annie let out a slow breath, rubbing her chilled hands up and down her arms. Tension carved a line between Swift's brows.

"Well," he murmured, "that went well."

"About as well as poking a wasp nest with a breadstick," Annie muttered.

They stood there a moment, and Annie let her thoughts reorder themselves, clicking into place like puzzle pieces she couldn't quite see the full picture of yet.

"Joe," she said quietly, "this is getting too tangled."

Swift huffed a humourless laugh. "That's one way to put it."

"No, look, let's just take stock for a second." She scrubbed her hands down her face. "Last night, Agatha raised thousands for charity."

"Which suggests she wanted the world to believe everything was fine," Swift added.

"And maybe it isn't." Annie nodded. "Everyone left then the lights went out, a tree fell and cut us off from the outside world in more ways than one. The chef is murdered. Theo thinks that chef wasn't even Soren Vale at all. Either he's right and we've got an impostor with a motive—"

"—or Theo's throwing sand in our eyes," Swift finished.

"Right. Then we find out Peter and Alice are the only staff left. Two people trying to keep this entire place running? That doesn't scream 'wealthy estate' to me."

Swift's jaw tightened. "And Noah. We still don't know where he is."

"He wanted to tell you something," Annie said. "But then he vanished mid meal, and his stuff was hidden in an office."

Swift's eyes shadowed. "I should have taken the time to talk to him before we sat to eat.

"Oi," Annie snapped softly. "No. You don't get to blame yourself for other people's secrets."

He almost smiled and Annie pressed on, ticking down the list in her head. "Then we read Noah's notebook—his research into Agatha's finances, the loans, the trust fund collapse, the legal mess over ownership. I think he was onto something and maybe Agatha didn't like what she saw."

"And now Agatha's missing." Swift said it flatly, but Annie heard the dread under the words.

"Exactly." Annie blew out a breath that misted in the cold room. "So, we've got a missing writer, a murdered chef—possibly an impostor—a missing aristocrat, two staff who look like they're hiding something, and two guests who snuck out in the middle of the night."

"And no phones," Swift muttered. "No way to contact the outside world. I can't imagine the tree has been moved yet and if it took out all the power lines then we're still screwed."

"Maybe the signal's back though," Annie stiffened, thinking of her phone laid out on the table in the drawing room with Noah's notebook. What if Tink and Page had replied and help was on its way? "Joe, we need to check my phone."

They moved at once, down the hall, down the staircase, the sense of urgency snapped at Annie's nerves like electric wire.

"Phones first," Swift said as they descended. "Maybe the signal's back. We need to make sure Tink and Page got that message."

"And then the notebook," Annie added, breath puffing white in the air. "We need to read it again. There have to be more clues in there about what Noah found."

They hit the bottom step and moved fast towards the drawing room door. Annie's heart thudded in her ribs with the excitement that she'd have a message from her team and they might be on their way to help.

They practically ran the final stretch of corridor. As Swift shoved open the drawing-room door, a wave of warm, yeasty air rolled out to meet them. Coffee and porridge, thick and comforting, and for one brief, disarming second Annie felt her knees wobble with relief.

Bea and Colin were already tucking in, the colour slowly returning to their faces. Theo sat hunched near the fire, hands cupped around a steaming mug of coffee. But Annie didn't stop for any of it as she headed straight for the little table by the window.

Her phone lay exactly where she'd left it, screen black. She snatched it up, thumb swiping instinctively and her stomach dropped to her feet with a sickening thud. Still nothing. No bars. No signal. No reply from Tink or Page.

"Damn it," she breathed. "Come on."

Swift hovered beside her, tension radiating off him. "Nothing?"

"The networks must still be down," Annie muttered, forcing down the disappointment that clawed at her. "But at least—"

Her gaze drifted to the place where Noah's notebook had been sitting. Except it wasn't there anymore. The table was bare.

"Oh no," she whispered.

Swift followed her gaze and his whole body went still.

"It was right there," Annie said, her voice thin. "It was right there when we ran upstairs. I put it down. I remember exactly where it was."

"Someone's taken it," Swift added grimly.

Annie's stomach dropped through the floor. She looked around. Someone in this room, someone warm and fed and sitting by the damn fire had seen that notebook and taken it when she and Swift ran upstairs to help Agatha. Then her eyes snatched on the roaring flames and there, right at the centre, was what was left of Noah's notebook.

"Who?" she breathed. "Joe, who would've—"

Annie's pulse hammered as she slowly took in everyone in turn. Bea and Colin, chatting softly over porridge. Theo, pale and hollow-eyed, staring into his mug. Peter and Alice, moving about the room with sad, tight-lipped efficiency. And Cassie? Had she come back in when she'd fled from them? Where was she now?

But Annie already knew, deep in her bones that whatever was happening in Blackthorn Hall, they were chasing three steps behind it.

FOURTEEN

THE SIGHT OF NOAH'S NOTEBOOK CURLING AND blackening in the fire, the only real clue they'd had, gone, snapped something in Annie's chest. A cord pulled too tight, a violin string twanged until it snapped. Before Swift had even fully registered what she'd pointed out, Annie snatched up the nearest mug of coffee, and strode to the door.

"Annie, what are you doing?" Swift called after her.

She didn't look back.

"Annie! Wait—"

But his voice bounced uselessly off her shoulders. She slammed the drawing-room door closed behind her, the sound shuddering through the corridor like a shot. She needed air. She needed space. She needed out from under the watch of those people before she said something she couldn't take back, or before the suffocating heat and tension in that room swallowed her whole.

Her stupid shoes clipped hard against the floor as she marched down the hall, coffee sloshing dangerously close to the rim, her breath tight and fast in her chest. She pushed through the first door she came to, the narrow one leading into the back of the house, letting it thud shut behind her. The sudden dimness was a relief. No polished antiques, no forced warmth, no eyes tracking her. Just a normalish corridor that smelled faintly of bleach and wood polish.

Annie strode through it, and shouldered open the swing door into the kitchen, trying not to look at the spot where they'd dragged Vale's body in out of the storm, the memory of his dead weight pulling at her.

She crossed the flagged floor quickly, her free hand lifting to the row of hooks on the wall. An old wax coat hung there among a few tired aprons, cracked at the seams, collar frayed, but thick and heavy and exactly what she needed. She tugged it down and slipped her arms through the sleeves. The lining was cold, but it started to warm her core almost instantly.

She pulled at the back door, and stepped out into the brittle morning cold. Pulling the coat around her shoulders, she let the door fall shut behind her with a solid, satisfying thump.

Then stopped dead.

The rear gardens, the manicured lawns she'd admired from the dining room the night before, were unrecognisable. A fully-grown oak lay splintered across the lawn like a fallen giant, its roots ripped out of the earth and pointing towards the sky like twisted claws. The conservatory attached to the west wing had shattered completely, its white frame crumpled and glass glinting like ice across the wreckage. The rose bushes were flattened; leaves plastered to the ground. Half the hedge had been torn open; the bare skeletal roots exposed as though the storm had peeled the garden apart to see what was inside.

It didn't look like a mere storm had passed through. It looked like the aftermath of a tornado.

Annie hugged the mug against her ribs and sucked in the cold air until it burned her lungs. Everything inside her was tight, the anger, fear, bone-deep fatigue clamped together like rusted machinery.

God. If she and Swift had just stayed home last night. Fish and chip Friday like normal with Sunday the cat wedged between them on the sofa, pretending he loved them when really, he was just after a scrap of cod. They'd have gone to bed smelling of vinegar and salt, slept like the dead, and woken up on a lazy Saturday morning the way they always did. Swift reading whatever hardback he was lugging through, Annie skimming the papers, both of them drinking actual good coffee, not the lukewarm dishwater she was clutching now. They wouldn't have bothered getting dressed until noon. There would be no bodies to deal with, no missing aristocrats, no impossibly impostor chefs.

She took a sip of the dishwater and grimaced, though a thought twisted sideways in her chest almost immediately. What if it hadn't been them here? What if Swift's parents had come instead? Would they have survived the night on a draughty sofa like Bea and Colin? Annie had never met them but she knew they were in their seventies too. Would they have managed without heat, sleep, medication? Would they have endured all of this as well as she and Swift had?

Annie's throat tightened, guilt cutting sharp and fast through her anger. She was being selfish. Yes, she was exhausted. Yes, she was scared. But she and Swift were better equipped for this kind of thing, seeing as they spent a lot of time in similar situations for work. His parents, not so much. Just as Bea and Colin weren't either, they looked brittle as matchsticks this morning, hollow-cheeked and grey under the eyes. If the storm itself hadn't nearly done them in, the stress of the last twelve hours almost had.

Annie looked out over the ruined gardens and breathed slowly, forcing the cold into her lungs as though she could freeze the panic out of her.

"Pull yourself together," she muttered into the steam rising from the mug. "This isn't about you."

Her phone buzzed violently where she'd shoved it into her bra and Annie nearly threw the coffee in shock.

"Jesus Christ," she gasped, grabbing at her chest. "Bloody hell, warn a woman next time."

She fumbled the phone free with cold hands,

breath puffing out in pale clouds as she woke the screen and saw, at last, a message.

MCU:

Tink: We got your text. Roads still blocked. Power lines down across the A-road and not safe to pass. Emergency services are everywhere. We're doing everything we can.

Annie's breath left her in a rush as more messages loaded slowly, pulling themselves through the patchy signal like they were salmon swimming upstream.

Page: We're trying to get a team in on foot but it might take a couple of hours as we're not sure what lines are live so it's not safe atm. Stay put and stay safe. We're coming.

Annie stared at the screen, tears stinging her vision. Finally, finally, someone knew they were trapped and help was on the way. She wiped away the tears with the back of her hand and then typed as fast as her cold fingers would allow.

Annie: Look into Soren Vale, pic from last txt. London chef. Something off about him. Might not be who he says he is. Will update when can.

She hit send and watched as the message spun, hung for a heartbeat then went grey with a single tick.

Just as it doubled the bars vanished and the signal died.

"Please," she muttered, letting out a humourless laugh. "Please don't be long."

She lifted her gaze to the sky. It was painfully blue and deceptively calm after last night's violence, the sun already catching on the shattered glass in the conservatory, turning it into a thousand knives of light. A flock of starlings whirled across the horizon in a slick, swirling murmur. Tiny black shapes moving as one, rising, dipping, weaving like a single breathing creature. Annie watched them, tears springing back into her eyes. How easy they made that freedom look, just lift your wings and go.

A cold gust cut across the lawn, biting straight through her clothes. Annie pulled the coat tighter and closed her eyes, letting the birds' song wash through her.

"Wish I could fly away too," she whispered.

But the chill that crept down her spine reminded her, that there was no flying away from Blackthorn Hall. Not until they found Agatha. Not until they understood Noah's disappearance. Not until they uncovered who the hell Soren Vale really was. And not until they worked out which of the people inside was desperate enough to destroy evidence under their noses.

Annie took a breath, squared her shoulders against the cold, and turned back towards the house. She trudged across the gravel, shoes crunching, her fingers wrapped around the now-lukewarm mug. As she reached the kitchen door, she slowed, seeing light moving inside. She took another step, then stopped dead when she caught sight of movement through the rippled glass. Peter's tall, slightly stooped shape passed in front of the aga. Alice hovered near the counter, her hands working nervously at her apron.

Annie edged closer, careful to keep her shadow out of the window's view. She shouldn't eavesdrop but something about their posture snagged at her instincts. Their bodies were tight, braced, the air between them vibrating with tension. Inside, Alice said something, Annie couldn't hear the words, but the movements were unmistakably brittle as snapped glass. Peter replied in a low growl, shoulders stiffening, and Alice took two quick steps back lifting her hands.

Annie's breath stopped.

In Alice's hand was a knife. A long, narrow-bladed, unmistakably professional knife, and Annie's stomach dropped as she realised what it was. The missing knife from Vale's chef roll. Alice was gripping it in her fist, shaking, pointing it towards Peter as though she didn't know what to do with the fear tearing out of her. Peter reached for her. Annie tensed, ready to burst into the room, heart hammering so loudly she was shocked they couldn't hear it.

But Peter didn't lunge with intent, he simply stepped forward and, with slow, careful hands, wrapped his fingers around Alice's wrist. Like he was calming a frightened bird. Alice's shoulders crumpled. She let out a ragged sob as Peter slid the knife from her shaking grip and set it aside on the counter. Then he pulled her into his chest, his chin resting atop her head as he held her tightly. Alice's whole body looked to be shaking with the force of her crying. Annie watched as Peter kissed the top of Alice's hair, heartbreakingly tender.

Annie watched, frozen, as the hug slowly ebbed. Alice's sobs dulled to small tremors; her hands balled in Peter's shirt. Peter squeezed her once more, before easing her back by the shoulders. They stood there a moment, then Peter wiped a thumb beneath Alice's eye, brushing away the last of her tears.

He said something and Alice nodded. She made a visible effort to smooth her apron, drag her hair back behind her ears, and force her face into something like composure. Peter did the same, rolling his shoulders, straightening his collar, pulling his mask of dutiful calm back over his features. Then, almost in unison, they both looked at the knife lying on the counter. Annie held her breath as Alice reached for it first. Peter opened a drawer, pulled out a tea towel, and held it out. Alice wrapped the blade neatly, tucking the steel deep beneath the folds until no glint of metal could be seen. Then Peter slid the bundled knife into a lower cupboard, behind a stack of old pots, shutting the door with a soft click.

Both took a moment to collect themselves, inhaled deeply, and stepped away from the cupboard. Alice picked up a tray already half-prepped on the counter, steaming mugs, a fresh pot of coffee, and a plate of slightly lop-sided biscuits. Peter added a jug of milk, adjusted the cloth beneath the tray, and rested a steadying hand on the edge.

They exchanged one more long and loaded look. And then, as though nothing had happened at all, they walked out of the kitchen together, carrying the tray back towards the drawing room where everyone sat unsuspecting.

Annie remained outside, hand clenched around her own mug, blood buzzing under her skin. Staff always had secrets, that was no lie, but Peter and Alice's secrets were knife-wrapped-in-a-tea-towel ones. And the worst part? Annie wasn't remotely certain whose side they were on.

FIFTEEN

ANNIE LINGERED OUTSIDE THE KITCHEN DOOR FOR A few seconds longer, letting the cold bite at her cheeks just to steady herself. Her mug had gone completely cold in her hands now. She tipped out the dregs into the border before slipping back into the kitchen, through the staff corridor, and into the main hall.

She walked quickly, almost at a jog, heart still thudding from what she'd witnessed. She needed Swift. She needed to tell him about the knife. About Peter and Alice. About all of it. Reaching the drawing-room door, Annie pushed it open, bursting through hard enough that it smacked lightly against the stopper. Several heads lifted at once. And Peter and Alice were already inside, standing there looking like there was no care in the world. Alice was pouring tea into mugs and Peter was passing around a plate of shortbread. They looked the picture of composed, attentive staff. Nothing like the two people Annie had seen moments earlier in the kitchen.

Swift looked up from his spot near the fire, eyes narrowing slightly the moment he saw her face.

"Annie?" he said quietly. "You good?"

She nodded but Swift caught the unspoken words she was sending him across the airwaves. Annie forced air into her lungs, swallowing down the lingering image of the knife in Alice's hand.

"I just needed to get some air," she said. "But the gardens are ruined. The storm has left absolute carnage in its wake, come see, Swift."

Swift scanned her expression, reading her too easily as always. "Sure, it'll be good to go and see if the telephone lines are back too."

"Not yet, sir," Peter shot out his answer as though scared Swift was about to leave the room. "Lines are still down; I tested them myself a moment ago while I was out searching for Lady Agatha."

Annie furrowed her brow, not believing a word that man said.

"Still, Swift, come look at the carnage. We can also call for Agatha and Cassie and see if we have any luck"

Swift didn't look convinced, but he followed her out of the room, stepping closer, and lowering his voice. "What's up?"

Annie clicked the door closed and looked around. She didn't really want to go back outside, but they couldn't stay here in case Peter or Alice came out and overheard what she was telling him. Remembering the relative warmth of the office, she made up the corridor and stole inside.

"Annie?" Swift asked, when they were safely inside. "What's going on?"

Annie locked eyes with him, her pulse still unsteady. Around them the room sat waiting for her story, still as the eye of the storm.

"I saw something," she said, keeping her voice low. "When I was coming in from outside, Peter and Alice were in the kitchen. They looked like they were arguing but I think they're actually together"

Swift's shoulders straightened. "There's no laws against staff being in relationships, Annie. In fact, it's more common —"

"They had the knife," she interrupted. "The one that was missing from Vale's roll."

"What?" Swift said. "Are you sure?"

"Positive." Annie's breath stuttered. "Positive it was a knife, anyway. I'm not 100% sure it was the missing one, but you tell me, if it's not, then why did they hide it?"

"What?" Swift said again.

"Yeah. Alice was pointing it at Peter. She looked terrified. But then they just wrapped it in a tea towel and hid it in a cupboard. Then…" She gestured helplessly towards the drawing room behind them. "Then I walk in there and they're playing tea party like nothing happened."

Swift rubbed a hand over his jaw. "Shit."

"I don't trust them," Annie said, the words tumbling out now she'd started. "I don't trust either of them. What if they're the ones who killed Vale and who have done something to Agatha. They're probably lying about the phones being down and keeping us here under false pretences."

Swift didn't waste a second. He jogged around the desk, grabbed the old-fashioned receiver and lifted it to his ear. Annie held her breath but Swift shook his head, jiggling the cradle and pressing every dusty button on the base.

Swift set the receiver down slowly. "No dial tone. They weren't lying about that."

He crouched down to check the cord but it was plugged in firmly with no damage.

"But, I don't get it," Annie muttered.

Swift straightened, brushing dust from his palms.

"Annie, listen, I'm not saying you're wrong. What you saw was weird." He blew out a breath. "But we have to consider all possibilities before we start accusing staff who might just be terrified of losing the only jobs they have left."

Annie pressed her lips together. "Terrified people don't usually hide knives."

"No," Swift countered gently. "But what if they think having it will make them look guilty. Or if they found it somewhere they shouldn't have." He leaned against the desk, arms folded. "We know they're understaffed and overworked. Probably underpaid given the state of Agatha's finances. Those two people might be trying to hold this whole place together, right? So say they found the knife by accident, I'd be terrified too."

Annie hated that he was being reasonable. She needed fury right now, something simple and sharp. But Swift pressed on.

"And we can't ignore the obvious suspects either," he added. "Theo argued with the chef—fake or otherwise. He left the room in the night. He had access to the kitchen. Strong motive, wronged professionally. He's a chef and he knows his knives."

Annie nodded reluctantly.

"And Agatha?" Swift continued. "If the financial mess Noah found is even half-true, then maybe money troubles are the route of all the mess. Desperation, even. And Cassie…" He scrubbed a hand over his jaw. "She's in a new relationship. Maybe scared that if the story of their demise gets out then that won't last? Who knows."

"So you're saying it could be anyone," Annie said, exhausted.

Swift gave a humourless laugh. "Oh, I'm saying exactly that. Everyone under this roof is acting strangely. Peter and Alice included. But we need facts, Annie. Not instincts alone, no matter how amazing they are."

He stepped closer, his voice softening. "And the phones will come back soon. Storms like this don't keep everything down forever."

Phones. The word hit Annie like a whipcrack and

her eyes widened as the memory surged back hard and fast.

"My phone."

"What?"

"We got a text," Annie said breathlessly. "I got a signal just for a moment when I was outside."

"What did it say? Who from?"

"And Tink and Page replied," she said, heart beginning to race again.

Swift's breath caught. "And?"

"They're trying to reach us as quickly as they can," Annie said. "There is a lot of debris that's unsafe but they're coming, Joe. They know we're here."

Swift's entire posture shifted and the tension in him seemed to flow out his legs making them wobble under him. "How long before they get here?"

"A couple of hours maybe. They said the power lines might be live so they have to go slow."

Swift exhaled, chest sinking. "At least someone's coming."

"Yeah," Annie whispered. "I replied, asking them to look into Vale to see if we can work out who that man in the cellar really is. I think it sent but the signal vanished again."

"That's okay," Swift said quickly. "They know enough. They'll reach us soon and we can get out of this hell hole."

"Yeah," Annie murmured, though her pulse still

hammered. She exhaled once, hard, trying to slow it. "Okay. So, now what?"

"Now we find Agatha." Swift didn't hesitate.

"And Cassie," Annie added. "She legged it after our little chat and nobody's seen her since. Two missing Blackthorns at the same time? That's more than weird, right?"

Swift nodded grimly. "We need eyes on both of them. And we can't let the others wander about freely while we search. Someone burned that notebook. Someone here is terrified of what we'll uncover."

She nodded. Fine, she'd wait for facts and evidence and procedures. Easier said than done, though. They stepped back out into the hall and Annie drew a steadying breath before pushing open the drawing-room door again. Everyone fell quiet instantly.

"Right," Swift said, with authority. "We need everyone to stay here. Don't leave this room. Annie and I are going to continue our search of the Hall and try to find Agatha and Cassie."

Colin's brows knotted and Bea clutched his arm.

"Oh, heavens," said Bea, her voice trembling as though it cost her effort just to speak. "Can't we just go home now? We've had quite enough of all this. Surely the storm's passed? Surely we can leave soon?"

Annie's heart softened, just a fraction. They looked so small on the sofa, both wrapped in borrowed blankets, grey-faced and shivering despite the fire.

"I'm really sorry," she said gently, stepping a little closer. "But the roads are still completely blocked. The trees have taken down the power lines everywhere. Even the emergency services can't get through yet."

Colin gave a weary sigh, shoulders falling. "We only came for a nice dinner, and now…" He gestured vaguely around the room, as though words had run out for the madness of it all.

"I know," Annie said. "Believe me, I know. But you're safest here, in this room, with everyone together and by the fire. Swift and I will be as quick as we can."

Swift nodded firmly towards them. "Stay warm and if anything happens, anything at all, you shout."

Bea took his hand in hers and squeezed. "We will. Thank you."

Annie's throat tightened just slightly as she took in their drawn faces.

"Come on." Swift motioned to the door. They turned back to leave when Peter called from across the room.

"Sir, shouldn't we come with you as we know the house the best?"

"No," Annie cut sharply. "We'd appreciate you staying here and looking after the guests, please. They need you more than we do."

She watched their faces, trying to gauge what they

thought, but could see nothing but panic. Good. She needed them all to stay together; Theo would look after the old couple if Peter and Alice tried anything. Swift touched her elbow lightly, a quick silent *ready* and she nodded.

They left the drawing room, the fire's warmth snuffed out the moment the door clicked shut.

"Where do we start?" Annie whispered.

Swift glanced down the long hallway that led towards the service wing then back to the front of the house and the ball room they'd eaten in not that long ago.

"Say you're right about Peter and Alice, and Agatha is still in the house somewhere, I say we search the staff areas quickly first."

"Okay," Annie said, and together they pushed through the swing door. "Let's start at the back, kitchen first and move down the house towards the front."

They swept through the kitchen first, moving quickly and methodically, but there was no sign of either of the Blackthorns

"No one's been back in here since Peter and Alice left," Annie murmured. "Should we move the knife now, put it somewhere safer?"

"Not yet," Swift said. "If they see it's gone they might do something stupid."

Swift quickly checked the pantry, the utility room, and even the little side nook where Peter kept the mop bucket, but it was all empty.

"Right," Swift said, striding for the service hallway. "Cellar next. You stay up here; I'm just giving it a quick once over and you still look freezing despite the coat. Nice find, by the way!"

Annie smiled, almost offering to share it, but Swift was in a shirt and jacket and Annie's strappy dress definitely won that competition.

Swift pushed open the cellar door and thundered down the steps two at a time. He was only gone for a matter of minutes, before he shouted back up the stairs.

"Nothing," Swift called up, his voice echoing off the stone.

"Okay, so where the hell next," Annie whispered to herself.

Something caught her eye as she turned to study the hallway. It was the cupboard door next to the cellar. She'd barely registered it before, assuming it was a cloak cupboard or broom store.

"Hang on," Annie said to the sound of Swift climbing the stairs.

Her fingers curled around the cold brass knob and she eased the door open a crack. It was freezing. Much colder than even the cellar itself and a sharp metallic tang hit her nose and crawled down her spine.

"Joe…" she whispered.

Swift reached her side instantly. "What is it?"

Annie pushed the door wider, slowly, cautiously. It wasn't a cloakroom at all; it was a cold room. One of those walk-in, industrial-style meat lockers. Even without a window, Annie could see where frost laced the metal shelves. Overhead there were meat hooks, large slabs dangling from a couple of them, so fresh they were still dripping with blood. Massive, hulking shapes wrapped in hessian with thick ropes holding them in place.

But it wasn't the aging meat that turned Annie's stomach, because tucked in the corner of the cold room, half-hidden beneath a heap of heavy blankets, was a mess of long, tangled dark hair.

Cassie.

SIXTEEN

ANNIE'S MIND SIMPLY REFUSED TO PROCESS WHAT SHE was seeing. Cassie's hair, dark against the dull metal floor, the heavy blankets heaped over her small frame like someone had tried to bury her alive in fabric only to lock her in a freezer. For one paralysing second Annie saw only stillness, cold, and the echo of Vale's dead body downstairs. Then the blankets twitched and a faint, broken cry drifted from beneath them.

"Jesus, she's alive." Annie lurched forward so fast she clipped her shoulder painfully on the metal shelving. "Cassie? Cassie, hey hey, it's Annie. You're okay. You're okay."

"Cassie? Can you hear me?" Swift was beside her in an instant.

A weak whimper answered them both. Annie and Swift began hauling blankets aside. They were thick and heavy, ice-crusted things that clung to Cassie's body. Frost burned to her clothes and her skin. Annie's fingers stung from the cold as she peeled them back. Cassie was almost the same colour as the shelves. White, waxy, her lips tinged blue.

"How long has she been in here?" Annie whispered, fear clawing up her throat.

"No idea. Help me lift her, let's get her out of here before it's too late."

Swift slid his arms beneath Cassie's shoulders and Annie took her legs. She was limp, making it hard to manoeuvre her in the narrow space between dangling carcasses and slick floor tiles. The cold smell of raw metal and old blood was clawing at Annie's sinuses.

A shadow moved behind them and Annie's head snapped up just as a figure filled the doorway.

Theo.

"What the—" He stopped dead, eyes going wide. "Is that Cassie?"

Annie's pulse spiked. "Theo, what are you doing here? Why are you following us again?"

"I was looking for you," he said, voice cracking. "I came to tell you something, then I heard the noise from here and, holy shit." His face drained as he stepped fully inside. "Cassie, oh my God."

He reached them just as Swift and Annie managed to wrestle Cassie to the threshold. Theo dropped to his knees beside them, cupping the back of her head to cushion it as they lowered her to the floor of the hallway.

"Cassie," he breathed, brushing hair from her face

with a shaking hand. "Jesus, Cassie. What happened to her?"

"She's alive, but she's freezing," Annie said, feeling Cassie's cheek. "We need to warm her up. Now."

Theo nodded rapidly, but his eyes snagged on something behind Annie. He turned his head back towards the cold room.

"What… what the hell is that?"

Annie refused to look as Theo stared hard at the slabs of meat hanging from the hooks.

"That isn't any cut of animal I know," he whispered. "Christ, I can't even begin to guess what Vale was feeding us last night. To think he called himself a proper chef."

Swift shot him a warning look. "Not helpful, Theo. Not now. Let's move Cassie to the fire."

Theo swallowed and tore his gaze away from the hanging meat. Together they lifted Cassie again, carrying her between them like a marionette, and hurried her back to the warmth of the drawing room. Cassie's breathing was shallow and quick and Annie wasn't sure how much time they had to try and stop her from falling into a dangerous hypothermic state that only a hospital could help with.

By the time they reached the drawing room door, Cassie's chest was barely rising at all. Annie pushed the door open with her shoulder and Peter and Alice froze mid-step, staring at the scene before them. Bea gasped, a hand flying to her mouth.

Colin staggered to his feet. "Good heavens! What happened to the poor child?"

Theo helped Annie guide Cassie to the nearest sofa and they pushed it to angle it nearer the flames.

"Blankets," Annie ordered. "We need more blankets. And can someone get that fire going harder."

Bea reacted first, ripping the blanket from her own lap and draping it over Cassie. Peter disappeared into the hallway and returned shortly with two more which he tucked around the young woman, while Theo poked at the fire and blew the base, encouraging the flames to roar.

But Cassie made no further sounds. She wasn't even shivering anymore, which Annie knew was a dangerous sign. She kept watch on the frighteningly shallow rise of her chest as she crouched beside her and placed two fingers under Cassie's jaw, counting the faint, stuttering beats.

"Come on, Cassie. Stay with us. Stay with us."

Alice hovered behind Bea, wringing her hands. "Should… should I give her tea? Something warm? Would that help?"

"No," Annie said sharply, lifting a hand to stop her. "Not yet. She could choke if she's semi-conscious. But—" Annie's eyes darted to the mug beside Alice's elbow. "We can warm her hands with it. Heat will help her circulation."

Alice nodded rapidly. "Yes, yes of course. I'll be one moment." She hurried out of the room.

"She'll be okay, right?" Theo looked back from the fire.

"We're doing everything we can," Annie said, though fear curled cold and tight around her ribs at the stillness of the youngest Blackthorn.

Alice returned with a hot water bottle wrapped in a knitted cover. "This is the only one I could find."

"Perfect," Annie said, and slipped it under the blankets, tucking it against Cassie's ribs. "The heat needs to get to her core quickly."

Bea took Cassie's left hand, rubbing it between her own, and Colin took the right. Theo sat rigid by the side of the fire, poking it to stoke the flames, while Swift and Peter stood near the door whispering so low that Annie couldn't hear what they were saying, until Swift stole away to the corridor. Annie frowned but she couldn't leave Cassie, and she trusted Swift knew what he was doing.

Minutes ticked by and Cassie's breathing stayed so shallow that Annie found herself leaning in close just to reassure herself it was still happening at all. Then, inevitably, the questions started.

"What on earth happened to her?" Bea whispered, eyes shining. "Who would do such a thing?"

"Someone in this house," Theo said tightly. "It has to be. Who else is there?"

Colin grunted. "Well, someone left the room, didn't they? Twice, if I recall. Where were you, young man? Where did you go?"

Theo started to square up to Colin, but he looked

torn between fighting an old man and keeping the flame alight.

"We should not be accusing each other." Annie was surprised to see Alice was the one to say it.

"But we must consider it," Colin insisted. "We're trapped. Someone is doing these awful things. And someone keeps disappearing."

His eyes flicked to Annie pointed and accusatory.

Annie lifted her head sharply. "Excuse me?"

"Well," Colin said, spreading his hands, "you did vanish for quite a long time, my dear. Off into the gardens you say but anything could have happened."

Annie bristled at his words, but she understood his paranoia.

"I went to get air because someone burned evidence," she told him. "I was angry."

"See," Colin went on. "She was angry."

"And she returned looking shaken," Peter said quietly, eyes unreadable. "Forgive me, but that is a fact."

Annie stared at him, not able otherwise to bite her tongue anymore, especially now Swift wasn't in the room to witness it. "I was shaken, you're right. Maybe because I just watched you and Alice hide a knife in a cupboard."

Alice gasped and Bea froze mid-stroke of Cassie's hand.

Theo's head snapped towards Annie. "Knife? What knife?"

"Annie!" Swift was back in the room.

Shit

"What knife?" Theo repeated, louder.

Annie exhaled slowly. "It looked like a long, narrow-bladed one. Alice was holding it."

Alice flinched. "I—It wasn't like that."

Peter stepped protectively in front of her. "We don't need to justify ourselves to you."

"Oh, don't you?" Annie retorted. "Because we're missing a murder weapon that looks remarkably like the knife you hid. And now we've found Cassie unconscious in a bloody cold room. Forgive me if I'm not in the mood for your little secrets."

Colin raised a hand shakily. "Please. Please stop shouting. Cassie's right here. We need to focus on making sure she's okay."

The room fell into a thick, volatile quiet with Cassie's breathing rasped softly through it. But Theo wasn't ready to let it go.

"Look. Someone did this. Someone put her in there. Why would any of us want to hurt Cassie? Why?"

Peter's expression tightened. "Perhaps you should answer that. You were the one who vanished into the night with her."

Annie hadn't realised that Peter knew this fact. Had he seen them go off together? Had Swift told him?

"I told you. We went to the loo!"

"Together?" Peter said drily.

Bea looked up sharply. "Is that true, Theo?"

"Yes!" Theo snapped. "Yes, all right? Why would I lie. I barely know the girl."

His voice cracked.

Annie sighed. "Everyone stop. This isn't helping."

Swift nodded sharply. "Agreed. No more accusations until we have facts. Cassie can tell us what happened when she's properly awake."

"If she wakes up," Colin muttered under his breath.

Annie felt something hot and furious spark in her chest. "She'll wake up."

As if hearing the words, Cassie stirred faintly under the blankets, a small, pained whimper slipping from her lips.

Bea sobbed. "Oh, thank goodness."

Annie exhaled shakily and pressed the back of her hand to Cassie's cheek again. "Come on, Cass. Stay with us."

Theo leaned in. "Cassie? Can you hear us?"

Her eyelids fluttered.

"She's warming up," Annie said quietly. "That's good. That's really good."

Colin and Bea huddled closer, protective to each other in a way that cemented their long relationship.

"Wh—where…" Cassie's teeth chattered, the words barely forming, but it was enough to stop the panic bile rising in Annie's throat.

"You're safe," Annie said softly, crouching in front of her and taking her hand from Bea's. "You're safe now." Annie turned to Alice. "Can we have some hot tea now, please? Make it milky and put a good load of sugar in there too. Thank you."

Alice scuttled away out the room and Cassie tried to sit up, pushing against the cushions with a weak tremble of her arms.

"Easy," Annie said quickly, pressing a steady hand to Cassie's shoulder. "Best not. We don't know if you've hurt anything else. Just stay still a minute, all right? Let the heat work its magic and then we'll get you up and checked over. Does it hurt anywhere?"

Cassie's breathing rasped shallowly. Her fingers twitched under the blankets, then lifted, gingerly, towards the back of her head. The moment they brushed her scalp she winced hard and sucked in a sharp, startled breath.

"Cassie? Do you remember what happened?" Swift leaned in.

Her hand hovered there, her brow pulling tight as fragments of memory seemed to slide painfully back into place. Fear flickered across her expression first. Then confusion. Then something close to heartbreak.

"I was hit," Cassie swallowed, trembling harder. "It… it was my mum."

SEVENTEEN

CASSIE'S WORDS HIT THE ROOM LIKE A STONE LOBBED through a pane of glass.

"It was my mum."

A thick, stunned silence followed. The only sound was the crackle of the fire and Cassie's shallow breaths still rasping as though her lungs were struggling with ice crystals.

Annie exchanged a look with Swift as he lowered himself onto the coffee table in front of Cassie, bringing his face level with hers.

"Cass," he said gently, "I'm really sorry to ask while you're still feeling awful, but can you tell us what happened?"

Cassie blinked hard, but her eyes stayed glassy and unfocused. It took a while for her to start talking and Annie hoped that no one would push her; this moment in time was as fragile as a spider's web.

"I… I remember leaving you. After you asked me

all those questions, I was so upset that you knew about our money troubles." Her breath juddered. "I went to find Mum, to tell her you were digging where you shouldn't. And that I wouldn't talk to you anymore."

Annie felt the sting in that, but pushed it down. "Go on," she urged softly.

"I couldn't find her. I looked in the dining room then the snug, where I thought she'd be, anywhere she normally goes when she's avoiding people." A tear slipped free and ran down her cheek. "So I came back this way. I thought maybe she was in the kitchen. Talking to Peter or Alice to sort breakfast. But when I walked past the back corridor, I felt someone behind me."

Cassie shuddered so hard the blanket slipped from her shoulders. Annie moved to tuck it back in, making sure there was no bare skin on show to catch a chill.

"What did you feel?" Annie repeated.

"Like someone was watching me," Casse said. "I got scared. There's a killer on the loose, I had no idea what to do."

"What did you do?" Swift asked.

"I was going to hide in the cellar, then I remembered that's where… you know."

Annie nodded.

"So I headed to the kitchen instead, only she stepped out of the doorway and blocked my path," Cassie whispered. "She looked furious."

"What did she say?" Swift asked.

"She didn't say anything." Cassie's voice trembled. "She just grabbed my arm and said I needed to stop making things worse. I didn't even know what she meant. And then she pushed me backwards and into the cold room. But I pulled back." Cassie reached up again, fingers brushing the tender spot behind her ear. "And that's when she hit me with a pan, and I don't really remember anything after that."

Bea sniffed beside them and Annie saw her wipe a tear from her cheek with her sleeve.

"Lady Agatha did that? To her own daughter?" Alice whispered, but it was loud enough for the whole room to hear.

Cassie curled inward. "She must have put me in there. I don't remember anything after she hit me. Just the cold. So, so cold."

Annie's jaw set. She exchanged another look with Swift, who looked as though he was trying very hard to keep his expression neutral. Agatha was now not just missing, she was a violent, unpredictable suspect.

Cassie wiped clumsily at her face. "I know she hates my choices. But I didn't think she'd go as far as that. I thought she'd come around. I thought because of the clause—" She stopped abruptly.

"The clause?" Swift said.

Cassie looked exhausted but she continued talking. "The inheritance clause. The one in the trust." She drew a shallow breath. "If I get married, the Hall automatically reverts to me. No matter Mum's debts; well, the debts that dad left us with, actually. And no matter that she's not been named on the deeds. The estate becomes mine."

Peter's eyebrows shot upward. Somewhere by the drinks trolley Annie heard Colin make a low whistle.

"So you getting married would undo whatever financial trouble Agatha is in?" Swift asked.

Cassie nodded miserably. "Yes. That's what I'm doing on New Year's Eve."

Annie finally realised what Agatha had meant when she laughed about Cassie's choices. God, that felt like a lifetime ago.

"Christ," Theo muttered under his breath.

"I don't understand," Bea said, wiping her eyes. "Why would she want to stop you marrying if it saves the estate?"

Cassie's voice came out small. "Because she doesn't approve of who I want to marry."

Swift shifted. "Who is he, Cassie?"

Her eyes shimmered as she looked around the room. "Someone she thinks isn't worthy. She thinks he's beneath us Blackthorns." She swallowed, gaze darting towards the fire. "Mum wants me to marry someone rich, just in case the clause is somehow null and void because she can't help but interfere. That way we still have a safety net of someone else's money."

Theo went very still and Annie's pulse flickered uneasily as Peter shifted on his feet.

"Is he here?" Annie asked gently.

Cassie hesitated. And in that hesitation, Annie

saw everything flash across her face. The fear, the shame, the desperate tug-of-war inside the woman. She was terrified of what revealing his name might unleash.

Annie squeezed her hand. "Cassie, you're safe with us. Whoever he is, no one here will hurt him."

Cassie nodded faintly. "He's sort of staff."

Colin, predictably, looked scandalised. "Staff?!"

"Colin," Bea warned weakly.

Cassie pulled her blanket tighter. "He works with us sometimes. He's kind, and he makes me laugh, and he listens. I thought… I really thought she was softening. But then last night, something changed in her."

"Something like what?" Swift pressed.

"At the auction, she kept watching me and him," Cassie whispered. "As if she wanted to stab us with her eyes. She told me that I had no idea what I was doing. That I was going to ruin everything. She said I was being stupid and blind. And this morning…" A sob escaped. "She hit me. She put me in a meat locker because I want to get married to a man I love."

Annie swallowed hard. The whole thing was so much worse than she'd expected.

Alice came back in the room with a tray as Swift pushed himself to his feet.

"Annie," he said quietly, "a word."

As Cassie drank her warm, sweet tea, Annie followed Swift to the far side of the room, beside a bookcase sagging under Victorian encyclopaedias. As soon as they were out of earshot, Swift leaned in.

"I went to check something out earlier," he murmured. "I went back to the cold room because it was bothering me the way Theo acted."

Annie felt dread slither up her spine. "Swift…"

"I needed to see what Theo meant about the meat," he continued. "And Annie, he was right. I thought he was just posturing as a chef, but that wasn't cooking meat."

"Oh god," Annie breathed, realisation settling. "Swift, is it a person?"

"Yes." His voice dipped lower.

Her stomach rolled and she pressed a fist hard against her sternum. "Okay. Okay. We need to be calm. Who was it?"

Swift's expression barely moved, but his eyes darkened. "I don't know."

Annie grimaced "What do you mean you don't know?"

"It was skinned," Swift said quietly. "Skinned clean. Headless. Limbs removed. No identifying markers left. Whoever did it knew exactly how to make sure there was nothing recognisable."

Annie felt like she was going to be sick.

"So it could be anyone," she whispered. "Agatha?"

Swift nodded grimly. Annie shut her eyes for a moment, willing the floor not to tilt beneath her feet. If the dead body was Agatha's, then Annie's sights were firmly fixed on Theo. Not only had Cassie pretty much told them all that she and Theo were going to be married, Theo had appeared as if by magic, more than once in spaces he shouldn't be.

"Jesus Christ," she whispered. "Swift, we need to contain Theo, now."

"I know," he cut in. "I'm thinking of how. Together?"

Annie looked at the man by the fire, she'd given him the benefit of the doubt and was kicking herself for it. She nodded and Swift moved quickly, preparing to restrain Theo.

"Theo," Swift called and Theo looked up, instinctively wary.

"Yeah?"

"Can you come here a minute?" Swift asked.

Theo's brow creased. "Uh… sure?"

He rose slowly, brushing his hands against his trousers, glancing between them like he sensed something was off. Annie angled herself behind him as Swift stepped forward.

"What is it?" Theo asked. "Is Cassie—"

Swift moved first with a decisive motion. He caught Theo's right arm, pinning it against his side. At the same instant Annie grabbed for his left, pushing his elbow inward to lock his movement.

"Oi—WHAT THE—?!" Theo choked out, jerking violently. "What the hell are you doing?!"

"Theo, stop," Swift said through gritted teeth. "Don't fight us."

"Don't fight you?!" Theo twisted hard, nearly wrenching free, but Annie drove her weight forward, bracing her feet as she forced his arm tight against his ribs. "What is this?! Let go of me!"

"Theo," Annie hissed, "don't make this worse. Please. Just stay still."

"I HAVEN'T DONE ANYTHING!" he shouted, his voice cracking with panic. "Get—off—me!"

Chairs scraped across the floor as Bea shrieked and Colin stumbled upright. Peter took one step forward as though to intervene, then froze, unsure whose side he should even be on.

"Theo stop," Swift said, breath controlled but strained as he fought to maintain leverage. "You're being restrained for your safety and everyone else's."

"For my… are you insane?!" Theo thrashed again. "What is WRONG with you people?!"

Swift pushed him forward, forcing him down into the closest armchair. Theo landed hard, breath bursting out of him.

"SIT STILL," Swift warned.

Theo glared wild, furious eyes lifting to each of them in turn. "Tell me what's going on. NOW."

Annie's heart hammered so hard it hurt. Sweat prickled between her shoulder blades despite the cold.

"We'll explain in a minute," she said, hating the tremble in her own voice. "But you need to stay seated."

"Explain WHAT?" Theo spat. "Why you're manhandling me like some bloody criminal? I HELPED you! What the hell do you think I've done?!"

"Calm down," Swift ordered.

But Theo was shaking so hard, steam was practically rising from his head.

"You think I hurt Cassie?" he demanded, voice breaking. "You think I'd do anything to her? You're insane. You're actually insane."

He jerked forward but Swift pushed him firmly back down.

"We're not accusing you of anything yet," Annie forced out.

"The hell you aren't," Theo growled.

Annie didn't trust the words forming in her own mouth. She didn't trust anything anymore. Swift kept his hand planted on Theo's shoulder, his body angled like a shield.

"The quicker you sit still," Swift said, "the quicker we can clear this up."

Theo glared up at him, his chest heaving, but he stopped fighting. He wasn't calm, not even remotely, but he was still at least. And in the relative calm, Annie could see Colin as he clutched Bea's hand. Alice had tears in her eyes. Peter hovered uncertainly near the door, his face pale and waxy. And Cassie lay curled on the sofa, cheeks flushed with returning warmth, eyes glassy but open and staring right at them.

"What are you doing?" she whispered hoarsely. "Why are you holding Theo like that?"

Annie left Swift to keep their suspect safe and kneeled beside her.

"Cassie, we're just trying to work out what happened to you and your mum," she said. "We think that Theo might have hurt her."

Cassie face crumpled, confusion deepening into bafflement, then into something close to horror.

"Why… why would you think that?" she whispered.

"Cassie," Annie said slowly, "you said you wanted to get married. You said your mother hit you because of the man you love."

Cassie's lip wobbled and a tear spilled down her cheek.

"Yes," she whispered. "Yes, that's true."

"We think that man has hurt your mum, maybe for the way she hurt you."

"Okay, so why are you holding Theo in a chair like that?"

"Because they think it's me," Theo shouted.

"Why would you think it's Theo?" Cassie said. "I barely know the guy."

Annie frowned, looking between Cassie and Theo, trying to see if they were lying. But they both looked as confused as she felt.

Cassie's voice cut through the thick air as she turned to Annie and finally told her the truth.

"It's Noah. I love Noah."

EIGHTEEN

NOAH.

So Cassie was in love with Noah, not Theo. She loved the guy who had turned up to write about their family history and uncovered some secrets that could turn their world upside down. No wonder Lady Agatha wasn't happy about the pairing.

Still, was that reason enough to try and kill her only child?

Money could do strange things to people but Annie could not fathom how a mother could do something like that. She slipped Cassie's hand back into that of Bea's, giving the older woman a nod to take care of her, and got up. Her legs ached with the cold and the tiredness. But hopefully soon there would be help on the way and she could go soak in a long hot bath at Swift's place.

First, she needed to talk to him about what they were going to do with Theo, given he didn't have a motive now other than professional rivalry. But, turning to look at Swift, Annie saw that the colour had totally drained from his face. He was white as a sheet, the colour dropped out of his face so completely he looked carved from chalk. His mouth opened, but no sound came out. Then, abruptly, he pushed himself up from where he had been holding Theo and stood. The coffee table shoved backward with a scraping thud making Annie flinch.

"Swift?" she said, reaching a hand out to him.

But he wasn't listening. He can't have even been seeing the room anymore. His eyes were fixed on the door, but they were somewhere far away. And then he moved, stumbling for the door, breath cutting sharp and ragged out of him.

From the corner of her eye, Annie saw Peter move in Swift's direction.

"Sit DOWN!" Annie barked, and Peter froze with his mouth half open. "No one moves. NO ONE."

She couldn't wait to check if they'd understood, she needed to get after Swift. He was already halfway down the corridor; one hand braced on the wall. Annie sprinted as fast as she could in her kitten heels, skidding on the cold floor.

"Joe—Swift, WAIT!"

He didn't.

He bolted through the staff door and disappeared. Annie caught the door just before it slammed and slipped through it after him.

"Joe," she tried again. 'What's going on?"

But still, he didn't slow. He was shaking. Annie could see it even from behind. His legs worked on pure momentum, his shoulders taut with dread. And Annie's heart lurched as she saw Swift pass the cellar door and fumble with the handle on the meat locker. Annie was beside him as he got purchase and pushed at the door, letting a freezing blast of air slam into them both.

Annie's breath fogged instantly, her bones felt like they seized, but she took a deep breath and followed him inside. Anger clawed at her gut as Swift stepped up to the large hanging shape he'd been convinced was a human body.

The burlap-wrapped form swayed faintly as Swift caught hold of the rope, his knuckles whitening.

"Joe," Annie said again. "You don't have to do this."

But he did. He *had* to. Annie saw it in his eyes.

Swift dragged at the burlap and what was left of it ripped away, dropping in a heavy wet thud on the cold room floor.

The thing underneath wasn't recognisable as anything human, not at first glance. It was a torso, skinned clean, inner flesh marbled with ice. There were no arms or legs. Not even a head. It was just meat. Human meat.

But even without any identifying traits, Annie could tell that this wasn't Agatha. It was too broad and well built, she was a slight woman with no extra flesh to speak of. This torso belonged to a man; there was no doubt about that. And Annie had a sickening feeling that she knew who it was.

Swift stared at it, his hands hovered, not quite touching the flesh of his old friend.

"No," he rasped. "No… no."

"Joe…" Annie moved closer, her own stomach lurching. She wanted to pull him away, to block his view, to shield him from the cruelty of what they were both looking at. "We don't know who it is."

"It's him," Swift choked. "Annie, it has to be him."

His shoulders dropped, collapsing under the weight of a grief not yet confirmed but already settling like concrete. Annie stepped forward and rested her hand on his back.

"He was going to tell me something," Swift whispered. "Last night. He said it was important."

"I know."

"I told him it could wait," Swift said, voice cracking. "I told him to relax. That we'd talk later."

Annie closed her eyes briefly. "Joe. This is not your fault."

"If I'd gone after him—"

"You might be dead too," she cut in firmly. "Whoever did this obviously has no qualms when it comes to hurting people. Joe, you are not to blame. But we do need to keep this as untouched as we can. This is a crime scene, or if not a scene, this is definitely evidence. Can we do that, Joe?"

Swift's breath shuddered and his hands dropped to

his sides, utterly helpless. Annie felt panic nudging at the edge of her ribs. Not panic about the body, not now, but panic about Swift. The way his face had emptied and his eyes had flattened to something hollow and lost. She had to pull him back.

"Joe," she said softly but firmly, "listen to me. We can't stand here staring at him. We need to preserve what we can until MCU gets here."

Swift didn't move.

"Joe," she said again, stepping around to face him properly. She put both hands on his arms, grounding him. "I need your help. Okay? We've got to cover him back up. Keep the body shielded. I can't do it on my own."

He let out a breath that fogged in the cold.

"Right. Yes. Okay."

"Good," she murmured. "Breathe. We're going to wrap him back up the same way, that way if anyone else comes in here they won't contaminate the scene with vomit or try to drag him down."

Swift swallowed, reached down, and grasped the edge of the fallen burlap with shaking hands.

"Who would do this?" he said as they started to drape the material back over what remained of the man Swift had once known.

Annie didn't want to think about what kind of person would not only kill another human, but dismember and skin them. A niggling thought was brewing in her mind as she looked at the clean lines of cuts where the arms used to be, and the way the flesh wasn't damaged even though there was nothing holding it all together.

"Annie," Swift said hoarsely. "Look."

She followed his gaze to the underside of the torso, the area where the gluteal muscles would have been and it wasn't smooth like the rest. The skinless flesh was cleanly cut, yes, but not just from the removal of the outer tissue. There were sections missing. Neat, rectangular sections, cut out with precision. Almost like they were sliced away.

Annie felt her lungs seize. "Oh god."

Swift stumbled backward a step, revulsion washing over his face. "Those… those weren't caused when Noah was skinned, were they? Were they?"

"No," Annie whispered, noticing a few more neatly carved sections on the other side too. "They weren't."

"These are deliberate," Swift whispered. "Someone cut pieces out."

Annie forced herself to stare, to catalogue and think about what it was she was looking at. Her brain tried to spit out reassuring lies, alternate explanations but none of them held as strong as the sickening realisation she was coming to.

"Whoever did this to Noah, they knew what they were doing," she murmured. "I think these… slices were taken for a reason."

Swift turned abruptly, a hand clamped over his mouth as he fought the urge to vomit. Annie stepped to his side, one hand on the small of his back.

"I know," she whispered. "I know. It's horrific. But Joe, we have to start thinking about who could have done this."

Swift dropped his hand and turned to look at Annie with bloodshot eyes.

"Who?" he rasped. "Who here is capable of this?"

Annie dragged a frozen breath down into her lungs, the air like knives.

"Peter and Alice have access," she said. "They're in and out of the kitchen constantly. They know the layout of the Hall better than any of us. And they had the knife, Joe. They hid it."

Swift shook his head helplessly, like he couldn't hold onto one thought long enough to make it make sense.

"But would they do this?" he whispered. "Carve up a body like this?"

"I don't know," Annie admitted. "Desperate people do strange things, but these two look like they love their job, they wouldn't jeopardise having to leave the Hall, would they?"

Her mind spun, connecting threads she didn't want to touch.

"Unless Agatha asked them to do it?" Swift added.

"Yeah, all roads lead back to Agatha, right?" she said quietly. "If she was spiralling, maybe she wanted to silence Noah after he uncovered the estate's financial mess. Maybe she panicked."

Swift looked at her sharply. "People in panic don't

carve out neat sections of flesh with surgical precision."

Annie nodded. "No. They don't."

Her eyes travelled back to the hook where the skinned torso hung beneath the burlap, its shape distorting the fabric in grotesque outlines.

"But, what if Agatha wasn't acting alone?" she swallowed hard.

Swift frowned. "Keep talking."

"Think about it," Annie whispered. "What if Vale and Agatha were working together somehow? Or Vale and Theo? They're both chefs. They both know how to butcher meat. Sorry."

Swift straightened slightly, looking between Annie and the remains of Noah. His breath clouded the room, but it had slowed back down to a normal rhythm.

"Though, didn't Theo say something earlier?" Annie continued. "About Vale not being a proper chef."

"But that doesn't mean he killed Noah," Swift said, though the doubt undercut his voice.

"No," Annie agreed, her stomach cramped violently, but she forced herself to keep talking. "But do you remember what Theo said about last night's main course?"

Swift stared at her blankly.

"He said the meat that was served wasn't aged long enough," Annie whispered.

The words hung between them like a noose.

Swift's face drained of even more colour. "Annie…"

"Noah went missing before the main course was served, right?"

"No. No, Annie, no, you can't—" Swift recoiled, horror flooding him anew.

"I'm not saying it's definite," she said quickly, almost desperately. "But the timing fits, Joe. And the cuts…" Her voice shrank to a whisper. "This looks like someone harvesting specific pieces."

Swift closed his eyes, breaking. "Please don't."

"I'm sorry," she whispered. "I'm so sorry."

She placed a hand on his back again. He flinched, breathing jaggedly through his teeth. They stood there together in the icy meat locker, both trying not to collapse under the weight of what they were realising. That someone had not only killed Noah, skinned and butchered him with skill. But they had done something even more evil.

Annie felt the ground sway beneath her feet.

"Joe," she said, barely audible. "Whoever did this didn't just kill your friend."

Swift looked at her, shattered.

"They served him up for dinner," she whispered.

NINETEEN

Annie had no idea how long she and Swift stood there in that cold room thinking about the notion of eating human flesh. Seconds, minutes, maybe hours pressed thin as paper. The cold burrowed under their skin, sank claws into their bones and refused to let go. At some point, her own breath turned shallow and she stumbled back a step, her shoulder bumping the metal shelving with a hollow, metallic gong.

That pain and the sound was enough to jolt Annie into movement again.

"Out," she managed. Her voice was barely a whisper. "Joe, come on. We need to get out of here."

Swift didn't argue. He looked as if the marrow had been sucked clean from his bones. Annie grabbed his sleeve and hauled him towards the door, not an easy feat with her legs trembling and her stomach lurching dangerously close to emptying itself.

She pushed him out into the hallway and slammed the door shut behind them. The corridor felt warm by comparison, though it was still cold enough that she could see their breath. Swift bent double, hands on his knees, gasping for air. Annie pressed her back to the wall and slid down until she hit the floor with a soft thud. She wrapped her arms around her torso, trying to banish the violent chattering of her teeth.

"Joe," she said gently, looking up at the man she loved who was normally her rock. She needed to step up for once. "Just breathe."

He sucked in several uneven breaths, each one a shudder. Then he gagged.

Annie hauled herself off the floor, grabbed his arm, and pulled him upright. "Kitchen. Now. We need water. Or tea. Or something stronger."

"Right," Swift croaked, but his voice sounded raw.

He let her guide him and every few steps Swift's hand brushed the wall, steadying himself. Annie's heels clicked and her balance was shot, twice she stumbled and had to grab the doorframes.

They cut through the service corridor and barrelled into the kitchen. The sun cast a sickly, yellowish glow over the counters.

"Sit," Annie told him, pointing to a stool.

Swift obeyed without a word. And she filled a glass with water, spilling most of it over her hand because her fingers wouldn't stop shaking. She shoved it at him.

"Drink."

He took the glass with both hands like it weighed a ton, lifted it to his lips, and gulped until half of it was gone. Annie busied herself placing both palms flat on the counter and leaning forward, breathing through her nose. She wasn't going to be sick, she refused, but her mind kept taking her back to last night's dinner and the plates of meat so bloody, they'd laughed about chefs always cooking it rare.

She squeezed her eyes shut, forcing the thought back into the box she'd kicked it out of.

"Annie…" Swift's voice cracked behind her. "Oh god, Annie. We ate flesh."

"No." She cut him off sharply. "No, Joe. Stop right there."

He stared at her like she'd slapped him.

"You didn't eat him," Annie said firmly. "We didn't eat Noah."

"We don't know that."

"Yes," Annie said, stepping closer, "actually we do. Because we were basically vegetarian by accident."

He frowned, confused.

"Your mum's a veggie," Annie reminded him. "It was supposed to be her and your dad here, right? So we had the mushroom thing, remember?"

"Oh god," Swift doubled over on his stool and let out a sound somewhere between a laugh and a sob. He grabbed her wrist.

"It's okay."

"Thank god," he whispered.

"Thank your mother," Annie muttered, squeezing back.

They stayed like that for several seconds, leaning on each other like two pillars holding up a heavy roof. Then Annie's phone vibrated violently in the coat pocket, once again making her jump out of her skin.

"Bloody hell!" she yelped, jumping.

She slid the phone from her pocket and swiped it open. There was one bar of signal, flickering there and away again. This must be a good spot for it, given the last time she was out in the gardens.

A message appeared in the group chat and Annie opened it so fast she nearly dropped the phone.

MCU:

Tink: URGENT. Real Soren Vale found in hospital last night with severe poisoning. Not fatal.

Tox pending but stable enough to speak. He catered a private meal for a couple before collapsing. Getting CCTV now. Too coincidental to ignore so assume that the couple are suspects connected to Blackthorn Hall. Your dead Vale was run through RFR and is a known hitman who has done time for assault. Backup heading in on foot. ETA 45–60 mins. Stay safe.

Swift took the proffered phone from her and read it himself. His expression shifted from hollow grief to that of shock.

"The real Vale was poisoned," he said. "And our Vale was a hitman. Which means that the guy who cooked for us last night—"

"—was an impostor," Annie finished. "Theo was right."

"Agatha knew Vale," Swift said. "She must have done, given that she was the one who hired him. She must have needed Theo out of the way and in order to do that she needed to make his replacement a real chef. But she used that as a way to bring in outside help to off Noah. I bet she and the imposter Vale were the couple in question. And in doing so, Agatha assured that her daughter wouldn't marry Noah."

"Agatha is nuts," Annie said, looking around the freezing kitchen. "I wonder if she had a man lined up for Cassie all along? Do you think she's still at the hall? Either way, we have a connection now. Agatha, the impostor, and the poisoning of the real Vale."

Swift looked back at the kitchen door. "Agatha's behaviour. Cassie being attacked. Noah dead. All of it…"

"Starts to make sense," Annie finished. "Horrible sense, but still sense. And what about the notebook being burned, who did that?"

Swift handed her phone back.

"I'm guessing it was Agatha. She caused a distraction up in her bedroom so we'd leave the drawing room and she snuck in when we were all gone and threw it on the fire. She's doing everything in her power to stop people finding out the Hall isn't hers anymore and that she's drowning in debt. We need to get back to Cassie," he said immediately. "If Agatha realises that Cassie is still alive, who's to say she won't try again."

"To kill her?" Annie's stomach roiled. "Right. Move."

They hurried out of the kitchen, and back to the drawing-room door.

"Ready?" Annie whispered.

Swift nodded and she pushed the door open hard. Five sets of eyes stared at them—Bea, Colin, Peter, Alice, Theo—each frozen in place, their expressions taut and uneasy. Cassie lay where they left her, wrapped in blankets and propped slightly upright. Annie was pleased to see that she was okay and the colour was finally returning to her cheeks.

"We made sure no one left," Colin said, nodding sagely like he was doing good work and was proud but didn't want to brag about it.

"Thank you," Annie told him, trying to muster a smile. "I don't suppose there has been any sight of Lady Agatha has there?"

"Nothing, is everything all right?" Peter asked.

Annie ignored him, still not feeling 100% as though she could trust the two staff members who'd hidden the knife. What if they were all in it together?

Instead, she crossed the room to Cassie and let Swift reply to Peter's question.

"You okay?" she asked, squatting down next to the sofa and warming herself at the fire at the same time.

A thought jabbed at her ribs, that if Cassie had eaten the main course last night, she would have eaten flesh from the man she wanted to marry. Swallowing down bile, Annie swore to try and keep that a secret from Cassie for as long as possible.

Cassie looked up at her. "I think so. Thank you."

Swift moved around the sofa to stand behind Annie.

"What happened?" Bea asked him, nervously. "Why did you run out like that? You frightened us half to death."

Swift's jaw worked, but no words followed so Annie stepped in.

"We needed to check something," she said tightly. "A lead. And we have new information coming in from MCU."

A ripple of tension went around the room.

Colin made a worried sound. "Are the roads clear? Can we leave yet?"

"No," Annie replied. "But they're coming on foot. Should be here in under an hour."

No one looked remotely comforted by those words. Annie exhaled and scanned their faces one by one.

"Can I ask all of you something?" she said. "Last night, did any of you meet the chef, Soren Vale, properly? Has anyone had any interaction with him before the dinner?"

Silence was Annie's only reply. Bea and Colin exchanged a small, confused shake of their heads and Peter and Alice mirrored them.

"I only met him in the kitchen, remember? But I did say to you that I wasn't sure he was a proper chef." Theo looked faintly insulted.

Annie nodded. "Yeah. And it turns out you were right."

Every head snapped in her direction.

"The man we all knew as Soren Vale," Annie continued, "the one working in the kitchen last night, the one whose body we found in the gardens, he wasn't Vale at all. He was an imposter."

Alice gasped and Bea pressed a hand to her throat.

"The real Soren Vale is in hospital," Annie went on carefully. "MCU just confirmed it was a deliberate attempt on his life, but thankfully, he's going to make a full recovery."

"So who was the man we were working with last night, then?" Alice piped up from across the room.

It was the first time Annie had heard her local accent come through and it made her seem younger than her years.

"We think he was a man who was brought here to kill." Annie didn't mince her words this time. There was a killer loose in the house and they must have had help.

And that meant only one thing.

Someone in this room was lying.

TWENTY

ANNIE FELT HER PULSE BEGIN TO LEVEL OUT NOW that they were back in the drawing room. Or at least, as close to level as anyone could get after seeing what she and Swift had just seen. The fire crackled, casting flickering light across Cassie's pale cheeks. Everything looked almost normal, though nothing in this house was normal or safe anymore.

Bea leaned forward, fussing over Cassie's blankets, her voice warm and grandmotherly.

"…thank goodness they reached the real Vale quickly," Bea murmured to Colin. "And that the doctors pumped his stomach in time. Poor man."

Annie stood and left them to it, crawling around the sofa to Alice and Peter for some help.

"I don't mean to put more on you, given the circumstances," she said. "But why did you hide that knife?"

Peter's eyes darted to Alice, and Alice's to him,

before she pressed a shaking hand to her belly, so subtly Annie might've missed it if she wasn't watching closely.

"I'm sorry," Alice whispered. "We shouldn't have hidden it. I know that now."

Peter stepped in front of her protectively.

"We panicked," he said. "We… we were afraid of what it looked like. There was a dead man in the garden."

Alice nodded, swallowing hard. "If the police found the knife then we thought Agatha might get arrested. And if she was arrested then we'd lose our jobs and our home. There's nowhere else for us to go."

Annie's breath caught as the pieces began to rearrange themselves. She didn't trust them, yet, but the fear in Alice's eyes didn't look manufactured.

"We've lived here since we were kids," Peter said quietly. "This place is our whole life. And we can't afford to move again, not with—"

He broke off, but Alice squeezed his hand, finishing for him.

"I'm three months pregnant," she said softly. "We haven't told Lady Agatha yet. We were going to wait until after the auction. But when everything started happening, we panicked. If the Hall changes hands, we don't know if we'd be allowed to stay. And if the police thought we had anything to do with… any of this…"

Her voice crumpled.

"We can't lose our jobs," she whispered. "We can't lose everything. Not now."

Annie stared at them, absorbing all their fear and desperation. It didn't clear them entirely, not by a long shot, but it made them less suspicious of the murders.

"Look," Annie said, keeping her voice calm, steady, guiding, "I understand why you were scared. But hiding evidence is a criminal offence."

Alice nodded miserably.

Peter pressed his lips together. "We'll hand it over. The moment your team arrives. We'll tell them everything."

"Good," Annie said, looking at the rough puff group of people stranded in the room. "I wonder if you'd mind fetching some more tea and maybe some lunch for these guys, please?"

"Of course," Alice said, quickly.

Alice and Peter slipped out, practically tripping over each other in their eagerness to escape the scrutiny. Swift stepped in close to Annie filling the space the staff had left, lowering his voice so only she could hear.

"Annie," he murmured. "I'm going back out there."

Her head snapped up. "What? Why?"

"We can't just sit here," Swift said, his jaw tight. "Agatha's still somewhere in this house, and after what we think she did to Noah and Cassie," he glanced at the girl on the sofa, "I'm not letting her have another chance at hurting anyone else."

Annie's pulse leapt. "Swift, she could be armed. And we know she's desperate."

"Exactly," he said. "That's why we can't leave it any longer." He hesitated, weighing something. "Theo's coming with me."

Annie blinked. "Theo?"

"I trust him," Swift told her. "And he's strong."

"I'm not letting her get away with what she did to Cassie," Theo added.

Annie bristled, her instincts flaring. "Swift, she's unstable. She attacked her own daughter and we know what she did to Noah. I'm coming."

"In what world does any of that make sense?" He looked at her with a cocked brow. "She's dangerous so you're coming too. No way."

"Yes way," Annie wasn't going to take no for an answer. "Bea is looking after Cassie and Peter and Alice will be back soon. Agatha wouldn't try anything with witnesses. So I'm coming too."

Swift dragged a hand down his face and stared at Annie with his deep blue eyes.

"Oh man," he sighed. "There's literally no way you're staying here is there?"

"Nope."

"Come on then." The three of them headed for the door and Theo cracked it open, checked the corridor, then stepped aside so Annie and Swift could slip through first.

Swift exhaled slowly. "Upstairs?"

Annie nodded and headed towards the staircase,

her legs prickly and weak from the cold and the sickening truth she still hadn't digested. At the top of the stairs, they made an unspoken decision to head back to Agatha's disturbed bedroom, pushing down the corridor where portraits of stern Blackthorn patriarchs glared at them with their oil-painted eyes. Thick dust coated the skirting boards, making it obvious Agatha hadn't had the full team of staff in a long time.

"Lady Agatha?" Theo whispered, peering into the room.

"Agatha?" Annie called, following behind him. "Are you here?"

A faint banging sound answered from the en-suite.

"Shit." Swift was at the door in seconds, his finger on his lips cautioning the others to be quiet.

Annie pressed in behind him, her stomach whirling around like an empty washing machine. Agatha might have been older and smaller but she was a danger to anyone who got in her way. And they were about to do just that.

Swift waited until Theo and Annie were beside him then counted down from three to one on his fingers.

Bursting into the en-suite, Annie's legs almost dropped out from under her. Lady Agatha Blackthorn sat curled in the dry bathtub, legs drawn up to her chest, hands clamped around her knees. Ankles and wrists and her mouth bound with duct tape. Her dress was twisted, one shoulder bare. Her eyes were wild, unfocused, glassy, orbs darting around like trapped insects.

"Lady Agatha?" Annie whispered, kneeling down next to the bath and pulling the tape slowly from her bloody lips. Agatha's head jerked up. Her pupils were blown, swallowing almost all the colour in her irises.

"Cassie," she hissed. "Is she dead?"

Annie froze at the words and Swift crouched beside her, lowering himself into Agatha's line of sight.

"Agatha," he said gently, "it's Swift. Joe Swift. You know me."

Agatha blinked hard as if trying to glue reality back together.

"Swift," she repeated, but her voice was wrong. "You're that boy, Cassie's friend. Lord Swift. The boy."

Swift swallowed. "Yes. It's me. You're safe. But we need to know what happened. Are you hurt?"

Agatha's gaze flickered, sliding along the tiles, the sink, the floor, as though she was searching for something invisible.

"You mustn't find Cassie," she whispered. "She didn't mean it."

Annie's blood chilled.

"What do you mean? Cassie didn't mean what?" she asked softly.

Agatha looked at her sharply, and for a heartbeat clarity shone through the haze before it clouded again like fog rolling over glass.

"She *knew*," Agatha breathed. "Cassie knew. She must have done. She must have realised what he did to Noah." Her whole body trembled, fingers clawing at the air as though trying to grasp the memory. "Cassie killed him. She killed him because he killed Noah. She… she did it to protect the boy she loved."

Annie's stomach lurched sideways. "Cassie killed Vale?"

Agatha wailed, shaking her head. Tears leaked from her eyes, hot tracks down her frozen skin. "I had to stop her and I had to hide her. Keep her safe. Stop her doing it again. I thought I put her where no one could find her."

"In the cold room," Annie said softly.

Agatha's breath hitched, jagged and hysterical. "Yes. Yes. Somewhere no one would look. Somewhere she couldn't hurt herself or anyone else. But they told me she was dead. They *told* me—" Her whole frame spasmed with a sob. "Is she dead? Please. Please tell me I didn't kill my daughter."

Annie's heart cracked. Swift leaned forward, taking Agatha's tape-chafed wrists gently in his hands.

"Agatha, listen to me," he said, voice low, steady, utterly compassionate. "Cassie is alive. She's cold, she's shaken, but she's alive. She's safe downstairs."

Agatha's eyes went wide. A raw, wounded animal sound tore from her throat. "Alive? My Cassie is alive?"

"Yes," Swift said. "I promise you."

Annie drew a slow breath, letting relief move through her body, if only for a second. "Agatha, who told you Cassie was dead? Peter and Alice? Did they say that to you?"

Agatha's gaze jerked towards the door, darting, lost, terrified.

"They said—" Her voice wavered. "They said she was cold. Still. That she wasn't breathing. That I'd… that I'd done it."

Annie's pulse thumped painfully in her ears. "Who did, Agatha?"

Agatha's head lolled forward, but she forced herself upright again with a Herculean effort. "The couple," she whispered. "The ones who came upstairs. They told me. They said Cassie was dead and it was my fault. That they'd help me. That we had to hide. That we had to… we had to fix things."

"The couple?" Theo repeated, voice tight. "Which couple? Do you mean Peter and Alice?"

Agatha shook her head. "They said they knew what to do. They—"

But Annie didn't hear the rest.

A single, icy thought slammed into her chest so violently it knocked the air out of her. Bea's voice, soft and grandmotherly, murmuring near Cassie earlier: *"Thank goodness they pumped his stomach in time."*

Her blood turned to ice. Annie had never said Vale had been poisoned. Bea shouldn't have known he would need his stomach pumping. Bea couldn't have known. Unless they were the couple who had poisoned him in the first place.

"Oh god," Annie whispered, horror creeping cold fingers up her spine. She looked at Swift. "Joe—it's Bea and Colin, and we left them downstairs with Cassie."

Swift's whole body snapped taut.

"We have to move. Now." Theo surged forward.

Swift was already on his feet, tearing the last strip of duct tape from Agatha's wrists.

"Stay here," he told her urgently, handing her a pile of fluffy towels to cover herself in.

Agatha nodded weakly, tears spilling over her cheeks.

Annie shoved out of the bathroom, heels skidding on the landing carpet as she sprinted for the stairs. Swift and Theo thundered after her, every footfall a gunshot echo down the hall.

Please be safe. Please be safe. Please be safe.

They flew down the stairs three at a time.

Annie hit the bottom step, grabbed the handle of the drawing-room door and prayed she wasn't already too late.

But the sight that met her as she stumbled inside the room that had been their comfort for the past twenty-four hours, told her that her prayers were falling on deaf ears.

TWENTY-ONE

CASSIE LAY CRUMPLED ON THE RUG, HER HEAD twisted at an awful angle, eyes swollen half-shut and fluttering. Peter sprawled beside her, his hand still outstretched towards the tea tray as though he'd tried to catch himself. And Alice was collapsed against the sofa leg, arms limp, mouth slack, a faint dribble of froth trickling down her chin.

"NO." Annie darted forward so fast she almost slipped. "Theo, Joe—HELP!"

Theo barrelled in behind her and swore violently as he dropped down beside Peter. "Oh my god. Peter, Peter wake up."

"Check their pulses!" Annie yelled, dropping to her knees beside Cassie. Her hands shook as she lifted the young woman's head, turning it gently to check her airway. "Swift, help Alice."

Swift crossed the room in three strides and started

to move Alice gently to the floor, checking her airway and folding her into the recovery position.

Cassie's pulse was thready. She had been through so much already, Annie wasn't sure she would be able to cope with whatever Bea and Colin had done to her. From the looks of the three victims, they'd been drugged or poisoned.

"Cassie." Annie patted her cheek firmly. "Hey, Cass, come on, stay with me."

Cassie's eyelids fluttered but didn't open fully so Annie rolled her on her side and glanced over to Peter. The young man groaned faintly as Theo talked to him, he was alive too, and seemed more awake than the women. Relief and terror knotted in Annie's chest.

"Swift, how is Alice?" Annie called.

"She's alive. Barely." Swift had covered Alice in a blanket, casting her as a small figure, and was examining the drinks trolley. Lifting the lid from the pot, he bent and sniffed at it.

"This smells weird," he spat. "I think there's something in it."

"Maybe it's the same stuff they used on the real Soren Vale?" Annie asked, looking down at Cassie.

If it was the same toxin then would Bea and Colin have learnt from their previous mistake and made sure they administered enough to kill this time? She hoped with all her heart that that wasn't the case.

Annie's head snapped to the window as the sound

of a car door slammed outside. Swift darted across the room, peering out over the driveway.

"Oh, you're kidding me," Swift growled.

Annie made herself as tall as she could, while trying not to disturb Cassie, and saw a small, ancient two-seater roadster pulling away from the Hall in a fishtail skid, tyres squealing on the frosted gravel.

"They're getting away," Theo said, horrified. "We can't let them get away with killing more people."

"Not if I can help it," Annie snapped, sliding out from under Cassie and rolling her on her side. "Listen, you need to make him sick—*now.*"

"What?"

"Get it out of him," she barked. "Induce vomiting. Stick your fingers down his throat and make sure he brings up as much as possible. Don't argue, just do it."

Theo's face paled, but he nodded hard, bracing Peter forward and sticking fingers into his throat until a wave of heaving tore out of him. His retching echoed horribly off the high ceiling. Swift had Alice slumped sideways, retching weakly, bile and tea splattering the rug as she shook uncontrollably. And Annie did the same with Cassie, trying not to gag at the smell of vomit spilling from her mouth.

"Good," Annie said, dizzy with the smell, and the sheer animal panic of the moment. "Keep going."

Cassie's body convulsed once, twice, then another thick wave spilled from her mouth, splashing across the blanket. Annie murmured reassurances, anything to keep Cassie conscious and to take her own mind off the grim scene.

"We good?" Swift shouted from behind her, frantic.

"Again," Annie commanded hoarsely. "Make sure their stomachs are empty, get every last drop out."

Theo obeyed, grimacing as he coaxed a final retch from Peter. Annie did the same with Cassie, fighting her own rising nausea. Sweat prickled her forehead despite the cold.

"This is the best chance we've got," she whispered, half to herself. "Come on, Cassie. Come on."

Theo wiped his mouth with his sleeve, shaking badly. "What now?"

"Now, Swift and I go and get the bastards that did this" Annie breathed. "Can you stay here? Keep them on their sides, like this. They might be sick again and the last thing they need is to choke on it."

Theo nodded, looking as terrified as Annie felt.

"Go," he whispered. "I'll handle this. Go and get them."

The door banged open making all three of them jump.

"Police, anyone inside needs to make themselves known now!" Three silhouettes appeared in the doorway, bundled in waterproofs, their radios hissing.

Annie almost collapsed with relief. The lead officer, a young woman with red cheeks and a windburned nose, took one look and swore.

"What the hell?"

"Poisoning," Annie said sharply. "Three victims. We've induced vomiting, but we need paramedics."

The three officers rushed in, two immediately helping Theo, the other kneeling beside Cassie.

"What did they ingest?" the officer demanded.

"We don't know," Annie said. "But our suspects just fled the scene. We need to go after them. There's another victim upstairs in the master en-suite. She's alive and breathing, but unwell."

"Got it," the officer said, thumbing her radio. "Control, be advised, suspects fleeing Blackthorn Hall, requesting pursuit when safe to do so. Requesting paramedics, four victims, three unconscious. Administering aid now."

"There's no time to wait until it's safe," Swift cut in. "We need to go after them now."

"DI Swift, I didn't see you there, sir," another officer said sharply. "You can't give chase; there are live power lines out there."

Swift grabbed Annie's wrist, already running. "We don't need permission."

The nearest MCU officer moved to block the doorway.

"You can't go back out there—the storm damage—"

Swift didn't stop. "Move."

Something in his face must have convinced the officer, because she stepped aside and let them through.

"Keys," Swift gasped, as they ran out the drawing room. "Annie, where are your car keys?"

"No idea," she cried back. "Wherever the valet left them."

"Yes! Hallway hooks." Swift didn't slow up as they reached the entrance hall. He skidded in front of a small door and yanked it open, beyond lay a pile of coats that Annie did a double take over. If only she'd known this was here a few, bloody freezing hours ago. And a board of keys. She reached in and grabbed her Hello Kitty plushie.

"Here," Annie called, throwing them to Swift. It may have been her car but he was the one with an advanced police driving licence. "Thank god I'm a child or we'd have never found these among the masses."

Chances are they would have, given that most of the cars left were Agatha's and they were all posh cars with very obvious keys. Or not obvious, given that they had no actual key. But that was beside the point.

They sprinted out and across the muddy courtyard. Annie's hand brushed the stone fountain as they passed and she plunged both hands into the freezing water. The shock was instant and violent, up her wrists like a whip.

"What are you doing?!" Swift shouted.

"I can't drive with vomit on my hands," she shouted, already numb from the water. "I already feel like I'm gonna throw up too."

She shook her hands violently, flinging droplets, and they sprinted around to the side of the hall and to her battered old VW.

"Let's do this," Swift yelled, yanking the driver's door open.

Annie vaulted into the passenger seat, pulling on her belt as Swift turned the engine over with a sickly groan.

"Come on," he hissed. "Not now. Not now."

The engine caught and Swift slammed the gas. Tyres skidded, gravel spraying behind them in an icy spray as they gunned it towards the gate.

"Hold on tight," Swift muttered, gritting his teeth. "I am not letting them disappear."

The old VW groaned as it hit the soaking gravel at speed. Annie grabbed the door with one hand and the dash with the other, heart hammering so hard she felt sick all over again. They burst through the stone arch at the end of the drive and immediately skidded to a crawling halt.

"Oh, for *f*—" Swift slammed his hand against the wheel.

A huge fallen oak lay sprawled across the road, splintered branches jutting towards the sky like severed limbs. The trunk was enormous, blocking the entire lane and the verge. Live wires snaked across it like metal vines, hissing quietly in the cold air.

"No going that way," Annie breathed. "At least we know which direction Bea and Colin went too."

"Yeah, let's go." Swift swung the car in the only direction available to them, throwing them both sideways.

The tyres squealed and finally found purchase as the VW shot down the lane, suspension rattling as Swift pushed it harder than any sane person ever had. Annie said a silent prayer that they'd all make it out alive, the car included. The storm had carved scars into the tarmac that they bounced through like bumper cars. Branches littered the road, puddles had frozen into black mirrors, and entire chunks of hedgerow were strewn across the verge.

"There," Annie pointed ahead, her breath misting. "Look, Swift, look!"

A small blur of silver skidded around a bend far ahead, tyres throwing up the slush. It was Bea and Colin's ridiculous vintage two-seater, its back tyres struggling for grip.

Swift's hands tightened around the wheel until his knuckles bleached. "Got them."

"Careful!" Annie barked as the VW hit a pothole deep enough to swallow a cat. Her teeth clacked together painfully.

Swift growled something wordless and pressed harder on the accelerator. The car leapt forward, engine whining in protest but obeying him anyway. Wind screamed past them. Surface water whipped sideways. Annie tasted fear like blood at the back of her throat.

"They're going too fast," she said, watching the roadster bounce dangerously. "They'll spin out."

"Good," Swift said. "As long as they spin before they reach anyone else."

Annie gripped the dashboard harder. "Just don't let us spin too."

"No plans to," Swift muttered, his shoulders coiled tight.

Up ahead, the silver roadster hit a curve too fast and swerved, its wheels clipping a fallen branch. A spray of sleet shot into the air.

"They're losing control!" Annie shouted.

"Then it's almost over," Swift replied grimly, lowering his foot another millimetre.

The distance between the cars shrank, fifty metres, thirty, twenty. Swift made a split-second decision. He pulled the Golf sharply left, cutting across the inside of the bend, tyres biting into the tarmac. The car lurched, and in the next second they were alongside the roadster.

Bea's terrified face stared at them through her side window. Colin was driving white-knuckled and wild-eyed.

"STOP THE CAR!" Swift bellowed, lowering his window. The wind stole his words away but the meaning was clear.

Bea shook her head. Swift swore and rammed the accelerator. The Golf pulled ahead by inches and Annie saw it. Up ahead, half buried in detritus was a large branch.

"Swift!" she yelled.

He saw it the same second Bea did. Colin yanked the wheel hard right to avoid it, but he over compensated and the little roadster jerked violently, skidding sideways across the slick road, tyres screaming against the wet tarmac. The car spun once, twice before the back wheel caught the edge of the ditch.

The roadster flipped almost gracefully, rolling onto its side with a grinding crunch and slamming into the embankment. Mud and shattered bracken exploded around it.

"Oh my god!" Annie screamed.

Swift was already braking, the Golf shuddering to a halt a few metres ahead. Annie was out of the car before the engine had even died.

"Bea!" she shouted, sprinting to the wreck. "Colin!"

The air stank of scorched rubber. The roadster had landed half-crushed against the bank; the driver's side wedged deep into the mud. A door scraped, then forced open with a metallic groan and Bea tumbled out first, shaking, her hair matted with leaves and soil. There was a deep gash on her forehead that was bleeding into her eyes. She wiped away the blood with a coat sleeve and looked like she was going to cry.

Colin pulled himself out after her with far more force, slipping in the sludge before steadying himself. His face twisted, frantic and furious as he grabbed for his wife.

"Don't move!" Swift thundered as he caught up to Annie, his badge visible in his hand. "Both of you stay where you are."

Bea froze mid-step but Colin didn't heed Swift's words. He lunged up the slope of the ditch, his shoes slipping, but he kept climbing. Bea went after him instinctively, sobbing, catching his sleeve.

"Don't," Annie warned. "Don't take another step."

Colin's lip curled. "Get out of our way."

Swift reached them, planting himself beside Annie, one hand on her arm in case Colin tried anything.

"It's over," Swift said, breathlessly. "Whatever you think comes next, it's done. You're done. No more running."

"We didn't want to hurt anyone else." Bea broke. "We didn't—"

"Oh shut up," Colin spat, wrenching his arm free. "That's a lie and you know it."

Annie felt a cold, sharp stab in her gut as Colin glared up at her beneath the dripping fringe of his white hair. Rage simmered behind his eyes, but underneath it there was ugly, desperate fear.

He wiped his mouth with the back of his trembling hand.

"That idiot," he jerked his chin back the way they'd come, towards Blackthorn Hall, "Darren got too big for his boots. The hitman. That's his name.

Darren Price. Thought he was some kind of bloody artist because he carved up that… that boy."

"You're admitting it," she said quietly. "You hired him."

"Of course we bloody hired him," Colin snarled. "We had to. Noah was about to ruin everything. Everything that should have been ours. We couldn't let him get away with it."

TWENTY-TWO

Bea was bleeding. A dark ribbon of blood had cut a path down through her greying hair and she kept scrubbing at it with the cuff of her coat, her pale knitted gloves smeared a rusty brown.

"Colin," she whispered, throatily. "Colin, please—"

"Shut up," he snarled, not taking his eyes off Annie and Swift.

He looked feral. Mud streaked his trousers to the knee, his overcoat torn on a jagged bramble or twisted metal of the roadster.

"Colin." Annie kept her voice as steady as she could, heart still pounding from the chase. "It's over. You're not getting away now. There's nowhere for you to go."

"Watch me," he spat back.

Swift stepped slightly in front of her, badge still visible in his fist. "Colin Fanshawe, Bea Fanshawe, you're both under arrest on suspicion of murder, conspiracy to murder and attempted murder. Anything you—"

Colin barked a laugh. "Spare me the speech, boy."

Swift kept going, reading the old couple their rights as Colin jabbed a muddy finger towards Blackthorn Hall, barely visible now through the trees and sleeting rain.

"That place was supposed to be ours," he hissed. "Ours and our son's. Not that spoiled girl. Not Agatha's. Ours."

Bea let out a broken sob, clutching his sleeve. "Colin, please, stop. I need a doctor, we need to—"

"We need them to know the truth," he snapped at her. "We need to tell them what we were promised."

He turned back to Annie and Swift, lip curling.

"Lord Blackthorn begged us for help," he went on. "Came to us with his cap in hand, said he needed money or the hall would be repossessed. Of course we gave them enough to keep it afloat, they are our friends. Well, they were."

"You were the ones who lent the Blackthorns money?" Annie said quietly, thinking of Noah's burning notebook.

"Not just money," Colin snarled. "Everything. Years of everything. My work, Bea's work, our savings, my father's savings. We were told that in the event they weren't able to pay back the loan, the hall would be ours for our generosity, that when Lord Blackthorn died he would leave it to us in his will.

But what did we get in return?" He threw his arm wide, as if gesturing to the entire broken countryside. "Nothing. You know what Agatha said when we asked about the deeds? When we reminded her of the agreement?"

Bea's shoulders shook. "Colin…"

"She laughed," Colin spat. "Told us that her husband had made sure their daughter was looked after, hidden some stupid clause in the small print about the ownership being reverted to us in the event that Cassie married." His mouth twisted. "Because of that bloody clause, all the debt would be wiped clean. Our investment—our son's future—gone."

"So you decided to solve the problem by killing the man she loved?" Annie felt hot anger bubbling in her bloodstream.

"Don't say it like that," Bea whispered, hugging herself. "Please. We didn't think of it like that, we were just thinking of our son. Do you have children? You'd understand if you did."

Swift took a step forward. "Even if we had a house full of kids, we would never understand. What you did was hire someone to murder a man. And then you tried to poison an entire room full of people to stop yourselves from being caught. How did you even find a man like Darren Price?"

Colin gave him a nasty, pitying look. "You think old people don't know how to find men who fix problems? A friend of a friend owed me a favour and put us in touch. Darren had done time before. He was happy to work for cash and ask no questions. We said it needed to look like an accident."

"An accident?" Annie snapped. "He butchered him. Literally."

Colin flinched, just a fraction. Rain dripped off his nose and painted him a sad picture.

"We didn't ask him to do that," Bea whispered, tears spilling over now. "We thought he'd do something that no one would question."

"But when he heard there was a fancy dinner, he got creative," Colin went on bitterly. "He told us that if we could get him into the house as the chef, no one would question him being there. All he needed was to get Noah alone. Said he'd 'take care of the rest'."

Annie felt bile rise in her throat, thinking of Noah disappearing mid-meal, that hollow space at the table where he should have been.

"And in London?" she asked. "You poisoned the real Vale so you could bring in an imposter. You knew Lady Agatha had never met Vale so she'd be none the wiser, unlike if you got Theo out the picture instead. How did you manage to persuade her to change from Theo in the first place? Especially at such short notice?"

Bea swallowed hard, her hand still pressed to the sticky blood at her temple. "We told Agatha that Theo's food had been giving people stomach upset and that he was being investigated by the FSA," she whispered. "We just needed him and Vale out of the way long enough for Darren to take their places."

"Does your son know he was to inherit the Hall tainted by so much death?" Annie snapped. "The Hall was never yours if you had been as meticulous reading the small print as you were at organising the killing of innocent human beings."

"Innocent," Colin snarled. "Off the record, maybe. Lord Blackthorn wasn't as innocent as he liked to make believe."

"Wait, what?" Swift spluttered. "So you're admitting to having a hand in Lord Blackthorn's death too?"

"Colin!" Bea was sobbing now. She knew their time was up.

"We decided to take what we were owed," Colin shot back. "We might have helped the old fool along a bit, but he was a dead man walking for years. Why should we have to wait so long for what's rightfully ours? But then that idiot, Noah, dug into the accounts and found out too much. If he wrote that story, our son's future would have been gone. We hired Darren to take him out before that happened; we didn't plan on *you* being at the meal."

"And when Darren told you what he'd actually done?" Annie asked, her voice fraying slightly at the edges. "When he boasted about skinning your victim, about serving him up as the main course, what did you think to that? He served you human flesh."

Bea covered her mouth, a strangled sob clawing through her fingers. Even Colin looked green around the gills.

"He was laughing," she whispered. "He was laughing about it. Said we'd never forget 'the most exclusive tasting menu in the county'. I screamed, I thought I was going to be sick. What a horrible man."

A snort escaped Annie, she couldn't help but see the irony.

"You think?" she said, laced with sarcasm. "A man hired to kill people could have a horrible side."

"We realised then," Colin interrupted, ignoring her jibes, "that he was a loose end. A liability. He was never going to keep his mouth shut. That kind of man doesn't walk away from something like that without bragging about it to his friends. He'd have turned on us the moment it suited him."

"So you killed him too," Swift said.

Colin lifted his chin. Rain ran down the grooves of his face, washing streaks through the mud. "He slipped," he said.

"Onto a kitchen knife," Annie said. "Multiple times?"

He smiled and it was the ugliest thing Annie had seen all day.

The wind gusted, lashing rain into Annie's face. She shivered violently and realised then just how cold she was feeling. The events from the last twenty-four hours had taken their toll and the chill had seeped into her bones. She dragged her borrowed coat tighter around her body and made to move to Swift. She wanted this over with. But Colin rounded on her.

"We did what we had to do." His breath, hot on her face, almost made her gag.

"Enough," Swift cut in, voice like a whip crack. "You're done talking. Both of you, step out onto the road and keep your hands where I can see them."

Colin's nostrils flared. "You really think I'm going to prison at my age for this? After everything she took from us?"

"Yes," Swift said simply. "I do."

Colin's gaze flickered from Swift to the VW, idling a few metres ahead, exhaust steaming in the cold air. Then beyond, down the road, where more storm debris lay scattered. Something calculating slid behind his eyes.

"Colin," Bea whispered, hearing the shift in him. "Don't."

He grabbed her hand, fingers crushing hers. "Come on," he hissed. "We can still make it. We can find another route out."

"You're not going anywhere," Annie said, stepping into their path.

"You can't stop us," he snapped, his voice cracking. "I'll kill you too if I have to. You and your boyfriend both. We've come this far—"

"Colin," Bea choked. "Please, stop. It's over. Can't you see it's over?"

"MOVE," he roared, surging forward, dragging Bea with him.

Annie flinched back on instinct. Swift lunged, catching Colin's sleeve, but the older man twisted, surprisingly strong, yanking Bea to the far side of the lane, towards the verge where the water pooled darkest.

"STOP!" Swift bellowed.

"Colin!" Bea sobbed, stumbling after him, blood still running down her face. "You'll kill us!"

"We don't have a choice," he shouted over his shoulder. "We never had a choice."

A gust of wind slammed down the lane, vicious and cold. Annie squinted against the spray to where the old couple were running and she saw it.

The power line.

It had been sagging before, drooping over the hedgerow like a snake. Now, with the extra weight of sleet and the wrench of the wind, one of its poles gave a protesting groan.

"Swift," Annie whispered. "Look."

The top of the pole shifted and the line dipped lower. Sparks danced along its length, angry orange against the grey.

"Colin!" Annie screamed. "STOP! There's a live wire."

He didn't even look back. He and Bea splashed into the deepest puddle, their shoes sending dirty water flying. Bea slipped, nearly went down, and he wrenched her upright by the arm, hauling her forward another step.

Then the cable broke.

Annie saw it go in chilling slow motion. The

heavy black line snapping free, curling in the air like a whip, spitting sparks that exploded in the rain.

"DOWN!" Swift roared, shoving Annie sideways.

They hit the verge hard, rolling onto the grass just as the line crashed to the tarmac with a blinding white flare. It landed directly in the puddle at Bea and Colin's feet and the world went white.

For a heartbeat, Annie heard nothing but a high, vicious buzzing. The air stank of ozone and something far, far worse. She looked over the verge and wished she hadn't.

Bea and Colin jerked as if puppeteered. Their bodies snapped rigid, arms flung wide, fingers clawing the air. Light danced up their limbs in crawling, crackling veins.

"Oh god," Annie groaned, but there was nothing she could do to stop it.

It lasted mere seconds but it felt like hours.

Then the current found ground and the flare guttered. The buzzing dropped away into a horrible, smouldering quiet as Bea and Colin collapsed like their strings had been cut.

TWENTY-THREE

The cable lay across the puddle, still hissing weakly, tiny arcs of light skittering along its wet surface. Annie lay frozen where Swift had knocked her. She realised she was clutching his jacket and he was clutching her back just as tightly.

"You okay?" he rasped.

She nodded automatically, then realised he couldn't see that with her face pressed into his shoulder. "Yeah," she whispered. "You?"

"Ask me when my heart's stopped trying to sprint out my throat."

They untangled slowly, both pushing upright on shaky elbows.

Bea and Colin lay motionless in the road. Annie's instincts wanted to run to them to check their pulses, and haul them up to their feet. No matter what they'd done, they were still two human beings. But the wire crackled louder when the wind caught it and a bit of gravel skittered too close, sparking it alive again.

"Don't," Swift said, catching her wrist. "You go out there and you'll end up joining them."

Annie knew he was right. That didn't make it any easier. Even from here, she could smell the metallic scorch where the current had earthed through them. It turned her stomach. A shivering tremor wracked her shoulders, not just from the cold, but the reality of it all. The horrors layered over the hours. Noah, the fake Vale, Cassie, the meat locker, the chase, the crash and now this. Bea and Colin's bid for escape had ended in the same storm that had started everything.

Swift's phone buzzed in his pocket, the reception finally returning to the twenty-first century. He grabbed it with shaking fingers.

"DI Swift," he said into it. "We're okay. But Lord and Lady Fanshawe are deceased. There's a live wire still active across the lane. Do not approach. We'll make our own way back, just make sure this road is cordoned off at both ends, we don't want anyone else dying, or coming across the bodies."

The person on the other end was half static, half voice. "Copy. Engineers notified. Units en route."

Swift slipped his phone back into his jacket with numb looking hands. "We need to get away from this before the line shifts again."

Annie nodded. She couldn't stop staring at the bodies.

"Come on," Swift said, stepping close and putting

an arm around her shoulders. "We've done all we can here."

Finally, she let him guide her away. They skirted the verge, as far as they could from thc puddlc and the deadly black cable. Annie looked back, just once, and saw Bea's white hair stirring softly in the wind. She didn't look like a monster. But looks could be deceiving.

They trudged along the verge; wind ripped at their coats, and the rain, now a brutal, needling mist, stung Annie's cheeks. They reached a stone wall, half toppled into the field behind, and climbed over, careful not to slip on the slick moss. Annie's feet sank instantly into sodden earth on the other side. Mud clutched at her heels.

"Bloody hell," Swift said, breath clouding white. "The hall's just over the ridge. If we push across diagonally, we'll hit the back gardens."

"Assuming we don't freeze solid first," Annie muttered, her teeth knocking together.

Swift shot her a look. "You okay?"

"Yes," she lied.

He didn't argue but he pulled her close and they trudged forward. Annie leaned into him automatically. Their shoulders bumped with every laboured stride, but the moment his body heat bled through her coat, her thoughts snapped somewhere dark. Back to the drawing room, to Cassie's grey face, to Peter and Alice slumped over like rags.

"Annie?" Swift murmured, tightening his grip. "You're shaking."

"It's just the cold," she said. But it wasn't.

She could barely feel her legs. Every step felt like walking on pins. But none of that mattered because her mind wouldn't stop replaying every terrible possibility.

"What if we were too late to save the others?" she whispered before she could stop herself.

"We weren't."

"We don't know that, Joe. What if Theo couldn't get them to be sick anymore? What if the toxin hit faster this time? Bea and Colin had time to adjust the dose after what happened to the real Vale."

"Annie." Swift stopped them both, gripping her shoulders. "Listen to me. Theo had help from the officers who arrived. They knew what to do. They would've stabilised them."

"Would they?" Her voice cracked. Shame burned behind her ribs. "I should have realised what was going on sooner. I shouldn't have left the drawing room that time, not after everything—"

"And if you hadn't," Swift said sharply. "You might have been poisoned too. You saved all three of them. If we hadn't induced vomiting when we did, they'd be dead already."

"They could still die," she whispered.

Swift pulled her into his chest without hesitation, shielding her from the slicing wind. "And they could still live. Don't jump to the worst-case scenario, that's my job."

Her laugh choked into his collar. "I can't help it."

"I know." His voice softened. "But we're nearly there. Look."

She turned. The jagged roofline of Blackthorn Hall rose over the ridge behind a curtain of sleet. Through the broken tree line she saw flashing blue lights.

"See?" Swift whispered. "The cavalry has arrived. Paramedics are here. They've got them."

Hope flared small and bright in Annie's chest. "Right. Let's go."

She needed to see Cassie alive. She needed to see Peter awake. She needed to know Alice's baby hadn't been harmed by the poison.

They crested the ridge and saw ambulances lining the drive, their headlamps cutting fans through the misty rain. Officers moved around the entrance and as Annie and Swift stumbled to the boundary hedge, two welcome figures sprinted towards them.

"Tink," Annie breathed. "Page."

Tink reached them first, skidding to a halt, her huge eyes widening. "Oh my god, guys! You're soaked! And, bloody hell, you're freezing. Page, get them some blankets!"

Annie tried to smile in greeting, but her jaw was trembling too hard. Tink hauled her through a gap in the hedge, Page grabbing Swift under the arm as both of them stumbled into the driveway.

"Watch your step," Page muttered, steadying Annie too as her legs wobbled like a fawn's. "The slush is freezing up into black icy murder traps. God love the great British weather."

He laughed, but when he properly looked at them his face crumpled.

"Christ, you're both blue," Page said. He waved frantically at the nearest paramedics. "Oi! Two hypothermic idiots over here!"

"We're not—" Swift started, but his voice cracked from cold.

"We are," Annie croaked.

A paramedic sprinted over with two foil blankets already unfurling in the wind. "Wrap these around your shoulders for me, yep, just like that. We'll get you in an ambulance and warmed up just as soon as one becomes free."

Within seconds Annie was wrapped in a crackling, heat-reflective cocoon. Swift looked the same, swaddled in shimmering silver like a baked potato. Page looked at them and his lips curled into a laugh.

"You two look like the leftovers I covered up for my gran before I left the house," he snorted.

Swift turned his head slowly, fixing him with the most unimpressed stare he'd ever given anyone.

"Page," he said flatly. "If you knew what was offered up for dinner last night, you would not be making jokes about human edibles."

Page chuckled to himself as he tucked Annie's blanket up around the back of her neck.

"What was it?" he asked, coming back into view. "Some sort of weird offal that posh people pay over the odds for."

When Swift didn't reply, Page's laugh died mid-chuckle and his smile twitched on his face. Then dropped completely

"Wait," he said slowly. "Wait—*wait*. You're not joking?"

Tink's eyes went even wider. "Oh my god, you're being literal?"

Swift swallowed hard, looking like the memory alone might make him collapse. "Very literal."

"What the heck happened?" Page asked.

Annie tugged the foil tighter around her shoulders, shivering so hard it hurt. "Not important right now. Cassie, Peter, and Alice, did they make it?"

"They're alive," Tink said quickly. "Barely, but they're breathing and being treated by paramedics now. Paramedics said inducing vomiting saved their lives. Annie, Theo said you did that."

Annie let out a sob-laugh and shoved her hand over her mouth. Swift's hand found her shoulder through the blanket and squeezed.

"And Agatha?" Swift asked, his voice still pretty thin.

"She's alive too," Page said, running a hand through his wet hair. "Bit out of it, mind. She's already in the back of an ambulance. She's been cautioned for attempted murder, but she's devastated. She kept saying all she wanted to do was stop Cassie hurting anyone else. But Cassie never hurt anyone, did she?"

"No," Swift told them. "And I can't imagine she will want to press charges, will she? Given… everything else that's happened here this evening."

"Poor Cassie." Annie felt sick at the pain the woman must be feeling.

Tink exhaled, her breath a plume in the freezing air. "Honestly, you two look awful. Hopefully another ambulance will turn up soon and you can get to hospital for a once over."

"We're fine," Annie lied through chattering teeth.

Swift nodded, but it looked like his chin might drop off from tremors. "Fine."

Page and Tink glared at them.

"Yeah, sure," Page said. "And I'm the King of France."

"France doesn't have a king," Tink muttered.

"Exactly," Page said.

Annie laughed so hard it descended into a cough that wouldn't stop. The paramedic jogged over, clicked on a torch, and shone it briefly into Annie's eyes, then Swift's. "Ambulance is five minutes away. We'll get you warmed up and on some fluids and you'll feel better in no time. After a night like you've had? Count yourselves lucky."

Lucky. Annie wasn't sure that was the word. Not with Noah dead. Not with everything they'd seen and done. But then she looked at Swift next to her, Tink and Page trying to trip each other into a muddy puddle, Cassie being lifted into an ambulance across the drive, and Theo giving them a shaky thumbs-up from the doorway of the hall.

Okay. Maybe lucky. Just a little.

TWENTY-FOUR

For the first time in a week, Annie O'Malley was warm. Genuinely, gloriously warm.

Swift's living room was aglow with the soft amber of lamps and a flickering TV screen playing a late-evening quiz show which both Annie and Swift were secretly winning. Sunday the cat was curled up in a perfect ginger spiral on Annie's lap, purring so loudly the cushions vibrated.

And the coffee table in front of her and Swift was covered with paper squares, two steaming parcels of fish and chips open like treasure troves. Swift lifted a chip dripping with salt and vinegar.

"This," he said solemnly, "is medicinal."

Annie snorted. "If vinegar counts as medicine."

"Vinegar is basically a health tonic," Swift insisted, tapping the chip against her cheek. "Especially when paired with deep-fried cod. And, I will remind you, you're still technically on doctor's orders to 'rest up and eat well'."

"Pretty sure the doctor didn't mean this."

"He didn't specify *not* this."

Annie grinned, leaning back into the sofa. Her muscles still ached the kind of bone-deep fatigue you only got after cold shock and adrenaline overload, but it was a good ache tonight. A recovering ache. A safe ache.

And Swift looked better too. He was still pale, but the dark circles had faded. His hair, still damp from his shower, fell in loose, boyish waves across his forehead. And he kept staring at her with the softest expression she'd ever seen him wear.

"How's your battered sausage?" Annie asked, nudging him with her knee under the blanket.

"Delectable, as always," he said, winking.

He reached across the mound of blankets and took her hand. His palm was warm and rough and familiar. Sunday stretched in her lap, his claws pricking affectionately through the cashmere.

"Sunday says we're never allowed to go out on a Friday night again," Annie murmured, stroking the cat's ear. "He says it's time to heal."

"Sunday also says he wants more chips."

"He absolutely may not have chips."

Sunday disagreed loudly and Swift laughed, settling something inside of Annie. They ate in silence for a while, both watching the TV without really seeing it, both basking in the easy, domestic quiet that had become their trademark comfort.

After a while Swift leaned forward, elbows on his knees. "So, Monday soon."

"Monday," Annie echoed. "Back to the real world."

"You ready?"

"I think so," she said truthfully. "Are you?"

"Ask me after another portion of chips."

Annie flicked a soggy bit of batter at him.

Swift caught it mid-air and popped it into his mouth with a grin. "Don't challenge me. My reflexes are still elite."

She smiled reluctantly. "All right, Captain Heroics. Monday. MCU. How do you feel about it?"

Swift sobered slightly, running a hand through his hair. "Shocked, still, I guess. Losing Noah…" His throat bobbed, and Annie gently slid her foot against his calf under the blanket in quiet acknowledgement. "Even though I hadn't seen him for years it still hurts. But, I'm okay. Better than I was anyway. And I'll be a lot better once the case formally closes."

"I'm glad Cassie forgave her mum." Annie said softly. "They're going to need each other over the next few months. Especially as they're having to move out of Blackthorn Hall. Do you think it's fair that Colin and Bea's son will inherit the hall just because Cassie didn't marry? Seems a bit unfair given that his parents killed the groom-to-be."

"They're not moving out," Swift shuffled back in his seat a bit so he could see Annie properly.

"What do you mean?"

"I spoke to my parents and they're paying off the Blackthorn loan so Agatha can stay. That's why Agatha wanted to invite them in the first place. And that's why she wanted us to stay for a nightcap. Money."

"Is that wise?" Annie said, feeling a whole host of panic scramble her brain. "I mean, what if someone tries to kill us for the deeds?"

"Don't worry," Swift grinned. "My parents have written it in the small print that they're just to go after you in that case."

"Not funny, Joe." Though Annie couldn't help but laugh.

It felt good to laugh. It felt normal. Swift leaned back, stretching one arm over the back of the sofa. Annie shifted closer until her shoulder tucked under the line of his arm.

"Swift…" she started.

"Mmh?"

"You know your parents want to meet me."

His head snapped around so fast she startled. "Yes. They've wanted to meet you for ages."

Annie stared down at her hands for a long moment. Then she exhaled, slowly and deliberately.

"Maybe we should invite them for Christmas," she said.

"Say that again." Swift arched a brow.

"Invite them," she repeated, bracing for him to explode with excitement, and he did.

"You're only saying that now there's a hit out on your life," he laughed.

"Oh, shut up," Annie said, swatting him weakly. "I'm being nice."

"Mm-hmm," Swift teased. "Look, seriously, it was a gift, not a loan. They don't want anything from Agatha, especially not to give the hall to us. They just want her to stop having emotional breakdowns on the phone to my mother."

Annie snorted. "Fair."

"Anyway," Swift said, nudging her. "You said invite them for Christmas. I'm going to need that in writing."

Annie pretended to scoff. "Absolutely not. Spoken word only. I have to at least have the idea I can change my mind if I get too scared."

Swift smirked. "So it's official."

"Yep." Annie leaned into him with a smile she didn't have to fake. "Invite them. Definitely invite them for Christmas."

"I'd really like that," he said quietly. "And they'll love you. They really will. Only warning, Dad will try to hug you within the first thirty seconds of meeting you."

"I can handle that."

"Mum will give me the look if I'm not treating you right."

"That's a green flag, actually."

“And if you give Sunday more attention than them, they’ll pretend not to be offended but secretly text each other about it later.”

Annie laughed. “Perfect.”

Sunday purred louder, head butting Annie’s chin as if to demand attention now. Annie obliged, stroking down the cat’s back.

Swift watched her. “You look happy.”

“I am,” she admitted, warmth blooming under her ribs. “Are you?”

Swift reached over and tucked a strand of hair behind her ear. “More than I’ve been in a long time.”

Annie nudged him lightly. “Guess we’re doing this, then.”

“Oh, we’re absolutely doing this,” Swift said, grinning. “Fish-and-chips Fridays, MCU case files, near-death avoidance, parents at Christmas, the whole thing.”

She rested her head on his shoulder again. “The whole thing.”

Silence settled around them again, comfortable and soft. Sunday stretched, flipped over onto his back, and exposed his fluffy stomach in total feline surrender.

“Looks like Sunday approves too,” Swift murmured.

Annie felt her eyes flutter heavier. Warmth seeped into her bones, her fingers, the place beneath her ribs that had been clenched tightly for days. She didn’t fall asleep fully, she felt herself drifting in that hazy place where the worst was behind them and the future felt possible. The TV flickered and the rain tapped gently at the windows. Swift tightened his arm around her, kissing the top of her head.

"Next week," he whispered, "let's try to have a normal case."

Annie huffed a soft laugh against his chest. "Good luck with that. Normal cases don't exist for us."

"No," Swift conceded. "But I'm going to pretend so Monday doesn't seem so terrifying."

"Deal."

She closed her eyes for good then, letting exhaustion finally win. And Annie drifted into sleep with fish and chips in her stomach, a warm cat on her lap, and the man she loved curled protectively around her. All was well. And finally, it could end that way.

Thank you so much for reading **The Final Course**.

I've got some exciting news!!!
For my next release I'm giving you something a little different. A stand-alone psychological thriller.

THE LOCKED WARD

She can't remember arriving. And she's not allowed to leave.

When Mara Keane wakes up inside Highreach Hospital, she has no idea how she got there. Staff insist she admitted herself, but the locked doors, heavy medication, and terrified whispers from other patients tell a different story. As Mara tries to piece together the hours she's lost, one truth becomes impossible to ignore: someone wanted her here. And they're not letting her go.

Investigative journalist, Rowan Archer, is uncovering alarming reports about Highreach Hospital's experimental treatments. Patients emerging confused, altered, or missing memories altogether. Determined to expose the truth, Rowan follows a trail of survivors to find out what's happening behind the hospital's sealed doors.

Highreach Hospital promises recovery.

But some secrets aren't meant to leave the ward.

A gripping psychological thriller for readers who love Freida McFadden, Alice Feeney and B.A. Paris.

If you'd like to order you can do so at:
KTGallowaybooks.com

And fear not, O'Malley & Swift will also be back for their next adventure later in the year; you can find out more and order now
at:
KTGallowaybooks.com

THANK YOU!

Thank you so much for reading THE FINAL COURSE. It's hard for me to put into words how much I appreciate my readers. You're all amazing.

If you enjoyed THE FINAL COURSE, I would greatly appreciate it if you took the time to review on your favourite platforms.

You can also find me at www.KTGallowaybooks.com

ALSO BY K.T. GALLOWAY

The O'Malley & Swift adventures available to buy now!

CORN DOLLS

Their first case sees Annie and Joe on the hunt for a young girl who is missing. Snatched from her home during a game of hide and seek. Left behind in her place is a doll crudely twisted from stalks of corn.

FOXTON GIRLS

When a spate of suicides occur at prestigious girls' school, Foxton's, Psychotherapist Annie O'Malley is called in to talk with the students.

What Annie finds are troubled young girls full of secrets and lies; and a teacher caught in the midst.

WE ALL FALL DOWN

When a young woman falls ill and dies after a night out, her friends blame a cloaked figure that had been stalking them in the streets. A masked face with hooked beak, immediately recognisable as a Plague Doctor.

THE HOUSE OF SECRETS

With a lead on her missing sister, Annie and Joe travel north and rent a small cottage in the village where Mim was last spotted. Only, the village has a dark history of its own. The cottage was home to a family who haven't been seen in over forty years. Their things still packed away in the basement, awaiting their return. It's a macabre destination for the dark tourist, and the rest of the village isn't much more welcoming.

THE UNINVITED GUEST

Back in Norfolk and back to work, Annie O'Malley and DI Swift are called to an isolated seaside village and the exclusive Paradise Grove Spa. Renowned for its peace and tranquility, the spa and its staff offer the chance to relax and recuperate in a discrete private setting on its own causeway. So when a dead body turns up in one of the rooms with no clue to who he is or how he got there, suspicion falls on the secretive group of guests.

DEADLY GAMES

When Annie and Joe are called to the local park to investigate reports of vandalism, they begin one of the most harrowing cases of their career. The vandal is a scared young woman with a bomb strapped to her chest and a list of games she must play. As the games get more gruesome, the young woman has a choice to make; kill or be killed.

ONE LAST BREATH

After the distress of Annie O'Malley's last case, she's in need of a bit of rest and recuperation. So her sister, Mim, books them on a flight to a luxury all inclusive resort in Spain for a break. But what was supposed to be a chance to sip sangria and reconnect with each other after so long apart soon turns into something terrifying when a group of armed men storm the hotel and take the guests hostage.

VANISHING ACT

When the celebrated illusionist, Gabriel Mirage, is found dead in the midst of his own vanishing act, O'Malley and Swift are thrust into a realm where the truth is as elusive as the disappearing act itself.

CHILL PILL

Annie finally reconnects with her father, only for him to be arrested and beaten to a coma. Can she and Swift clear his name so Annie can find out the truth of her childhood before it's too late?

BLEEDING HEARTS

In the game of love, losing your heart can be deadly. When six bodies are found in an abandoned pool, hearts missing, O'Malley and Swift race to stop a killer with a twisted message. Can they unravel the truth before another heart is stolen

THE GHOST PORTRAIT

When renowned artist, Eliza Warren, prepares her final exhibition, one portrait refuses to stay silent. The unfinished painting of a woman shifts, her face twisting with a sinister life of its own. As shadows close in, Eliza realises her masterpiece isn't just art—it's a deadly secret waiting to be unleashed.

ESCAPE ROOM

O'Malley, Swift, and the MCU Team head off to a well-deserved away day in a luxury escape room. But the moment the doors are locked behind them, things start to feel off. The puzzles are cruel, the tasks are twisted, and the game doesn't end when the timer hits zero.

THE FINAL COURSE

O'Malley and Swift arrive at Blackthorn Hall for a charity auction and dinner, only for a brutal storm to trap everyone inside. When the chef is found dead in the kitchens, it's clear the night has taken a turn for the worse. With guests stranded and power failing, Annie and Joe must find the killer before he makes it their final course.

Stand-alone Psychological Thrillers

THE LOCKED WARD

Hospitalised with no memory of how she got there, Mara Keane is plagued by missing memories.

Investigative journalist, Rowan Archer, is uncovering alarming reports about Highreach Hospital's experimental treatments.

Highreach Hospital promises recovery.

But some secrets aren't meant to leave the ward.

Printed in Dunstable, United Kingdom

76092360R00151